AF260931

DEDICATION

This book is dedicated to the memory of my beloved mother, Jaquelin Caskie Burns (1920-2006).

Front cover: portrait of Vipsania based on photo of a sculpture from Leptis Magna, Libya, Tripoli Archeological Museum, Africa Italiana 8 (1941); copper coin with portrait of Gaius Asinius Gallus (courtesy Münzen & Medaillen GmbH) above copper coin of Tiberius (courtesy Freeman and Sear).

Back cover: brass coin issued by Drusus Caesar.

Published by:

Pietas Publications
Waynesboro, Virginia, USA
web: www.jasperburns.com
email: pietas@jasperburns.com

VIPSANIA

A ROMAN ODYSSEY

By Jasper Burns

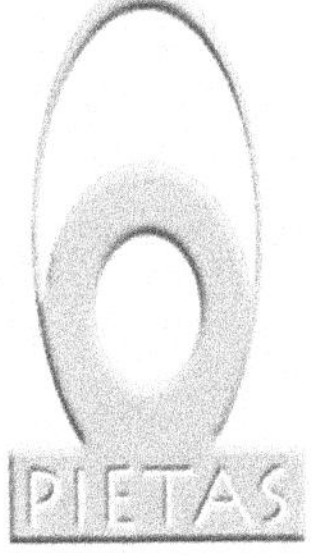

VIPSANIA

A Roman Odyssey

CONTENTS

"May the gods and goddesses destroy me, even more fully than I already feel myself wasting away each day, if I know right now what to write to you, senators, or how to write it, or what not to write at all."

Tiberius to the Roman senate, AD 32 Tacitus, Annals, 6.6
(translation by James R. Burns)

Chapter 1 – Tiberius the General (15 BC)

On the fringes of the Roman Empire, Rhaetian warriors had attacked northern Italy and the Roman provinces of Gaul. The barbarians slaughtered all male captives – even unborn male fetuses, whose sex they determined by magic.

Such atrocities were intolerable, so Roman armies commanded by the 27 year-old prince Tiberius and his younger brother Drusus pushed the barbarians deep into the Alps. However, the Rhaetians refused to surrender.

One of the enemy strongholds was on Lake Venetus, 33 miles long and walled in by impenetrable mountains on three sides. The barbarians were entrenched on its northern shore, their backs protected by towering peaks.

Taking this position by storm seemed impossible, so his officers advised Tiberius to move on to easier targets. Perhaps this bastion would surrender without a fight when the enemy cause became hopeless elsewhere?

Tiberius was not a reckless commander; he never risked his troops unnecessarily. But he also never made a decision before he knew all the facts. He knew that the failure to capture this fortress would encourage the barbarians, so he sent scouts to reconnoiter the enemy position.

Their report was not encouraging: 15-20,000 warriors were in the stockade, with their women and children. Massive fortifications defended the narrow passes on either side, making it impossible for the Romans to use siege engines or storm the fort with sufficient manpower.

Tiberius pointed across the lake: "And the beach defenses?"

The scouts looked at each other in surprise. One of them replied: "Nothing to speak of, sir. They know we won't attack by water!"

Tiberius glanced at Lucilius Longus, his second in command and long-time friend. They exchanged grins. Then Tiberius addressed his chief engineer.

"Build enough ships to carry two legions. You have three weeks." He turned to Longus: "Fortify the mountain passes on their flanks so they can't escape."

And so the enemy was hemmed in and the ships were built. The operation went exactly as Tiberius had planned - the barbarians were completely unprepared for the apparition of a Roman fleet on a mountain lake.

This brilliant maneuver was but one of many devised by Tiberius during his conquest of the Alps. It marked the end of this campaigning season and, while his legions dismantled the fortress and dealt with the barbarian captives, Tiberius mounted his horse and made for Rome.

Chapter 2 – Home for the Winter (15 BC)

Vipsania was spinning wool. It was dusk and the light in the courtyard was growing too dim for her to work. She watched the evening star come into view – a spot of bright silver in a lavender sky.

A cricket that had been singing from under a cedar bush suddenly stopped. There was the faintest whisper of leather on stone – it was her husband Tiberius, returning home from the German war! His cloak still covered his head, but not his smile, nor the grime and sweat that caked his cheeks. She was lifted by love into his arms.

After long kisses and longer caresses, Vipsania whispered to him. "You smell of horses and onions - let me bathe you."

They strolled to the baths. She removed his tunic and sandals and pulled him into the water. The dirt floated away and his body softened, then hardened with passion and they made the love they had dreamed about for months.

In an hour or two, the residue of separation was gone – they were one creature once again. He told her of his exploits in the Alps, where he had subdued the German tribesmen and punished them for their brutality. She told him of births in the imperial family, of her endless spinning, of his mother's compliments.

Then they were silent and remembered how much they had missed each other. Again, they welded their bodies together. Tiberius carried her from the pool to her bed and they slept like puppies.

Tiberius was the stepson of Augustus, the first Roman emperor. Since his victory over Mark Antony and Cleopatra 16 years before, Augustus had consolidated power in his own hands and brought political stability to the Greco-Roman world. He hoped to end the power struggles that had destroyed the Roman Republic by making his own family so preeminent politically that it could have no rivals.

Toward this end, he arranged marriages within his extended family and circle of friends and advanced his younger male relatives far beyond their years, reserving for them the most prestigious posts and assignments.

Among the emperor's protégés were Tiberius and his younger brother Drusus – the sons of Augustus' wife Livia and her first husband. At the age of 17, Tiberius had campaigned with Augustus in Spain. At 22, he was given his first important military command and was married to Vipsania Agrippina, the daughter of the military genius Marcus Agrippa, the second most important man in the empire.

Vipsania was only 13 on her wedding day, but almost a grown woman physically. She was tall and slim, with dark auburn hair and somewhat blunt facial features. She had her father's heavy cheekbones and ample lips, but her movements were graceful and her voice low and musical. When she spoke or smiled or laughed, her dark eyes sparkled and she was, almost surprisingly, quite beautiful.

Tiberius' features were aristocratic and appealing – a curving nose, pro-digious in size, but slender and well-proportioned. A vast forehead framed his large stern eyes, giving his glare the power to intimidate, even terrify. His mouth was small, but supported by a strong, slightly jutting chin. Lean and very tall, he was a head above the average Roman, with broad shoul-ders and muscled limbs, and he cut an impressive figure publicly. But less so privately, where he clasped his hands behind his back and slouched, like a schoolboy hoping not to be called upon.

After the very public wedding ceremonies, the young couple's life to-gether had settled into a melancholy routine of long separations during the warmer months, when Tiberius' duties called him to war, and glorious reunions each winter.

Their love blossomed easily. Both of them were introspective and some-what shy and a genuine compatibility ensured their happiness together.

During his absences, Tiberius wrote long, intimate letters to Vipsania. They were like diary entries, describing his every thought and experience. The relationship was not the standoffish sort so prevalent in the Roman nobility. Nine years older than his bride, Tiberius was a late developer emotionally. They were growing up together, and their correspondence kept them from growing apart.

Vipsania lived with her mother-in-law while Tiberius was away. In her early 40's, Livia was a striking woman with an air of self-assurance, even authority, but no lack of warmth. The resemblance to her elder son was pronounced – the small mouth, chiseled nose, full cheeks, aristocratic air. Her hair was reddish blond; her large brown eyes always alert and expressive.

Livia was a mentor to Vipsania, training her to fulfill her important role with dignity and grace. In truth, the instruction that Vipsania received surprised her. She expected guidance in the selection and overseeing of servants, perhaps some pointers on how to please Tiberius in her dress and the daily menu. But what she got was quite different:

"My son has a great deal of sweetness and talent, but he lacks ambition. You will have to decide what he needs to do in his career and make sure that he does it. I can help you now, but someday you'll be in my position as *mater familias* (mother of the family) and you will need to know what is necessary for everyone."

Vipsania's mouth fell open. Livia laughed gently and reassured her, "There is plenty of time, my dear. I will guide you. But this is very important; people envy our position and will do whatever they can to move us out of the way. Tiberius is not good at this game, so you will have to be."

The same advice was being given to Antonia, the wife of Tiberius' brother Drusus. The daughter of Augustus' sister Octavia by Mark Antony, she was a couple of years older than Vipsania. To their delight and relief, the two young women became close friends. They were similar in their tastes and temperaments, and devoted to their husbands, who were as close as brothers should be.

The greatest challenge for Vipsania and Antonia was dealing with Julia, Augustus' daughter and the third wife of Vipsania's father Agrippa. She was only a few years older - Vipsania never looked on her as a stepmother - but Julia took it upon herself to instruct them, and in very different directions than Livia.

To Julia, the role of a princess was to lead society in all that was new and fashionable; to be a public icon. She was soon disappointed by the demure and traditionally-minded Vipsania and Antonia.

And so Tiberius' life lurched back and forth, from the bliss of family life to the horrors and exertions of war. He and Vipsania made their home in a mansion that had once belonged to Pompey the Great, the rival of Julius Caesar. Mark Antony had also owned the place, and Cleopatra herself once paced its rooms, manipulating in her mind the men of Rome. Now it belonged to Rome's rising star.

The next year, Tiberius was home in time for the birth of a son, on the 7th of October. He was named Drusus, like his uncle, and, like most Roman babies, he was adored and worshipped to excess. When Drusus was one year old, his mother was expecting again.

———

It was a pleasant day in late March. The young family was in the garden courtyard, nibbling an afternoon snack of cucumbers, olives, soft cheeses, and bread, the servants orbiting from a distance. Vipsania selected the softest bits of cheese and un-crusted bread for Drusus to taste.

Tiberius moaned with pleasure as he ate a cucumber. Vipsania teased him: "How do you survive in the Alps without your cucumbers? I believe you love them more than you love me!"

Tiberius was silent.

Vipsania laughed; smacked him playfully on the shoulder. She felt her baby kick and placed her hand on her swollen belly. Tiberius noticed and smiled.

He presented her with a necklace – a Trojan horse in red carnelian, dangling from a silken cord. She was surprised; delighted. She fingered the horse quizzically.

Tiberius explained: "There is a Ulysses within you as well. I know it." He placed it around her neck.

"But why now?"

Tiberius pretended to be crushed. "You have forgotten our anniversary?"

"Our what?"

"Twenty years ago, we were betrothed to each other... (looking hurt) and it meant so little to you!"

Vipsania stroked his chin. "I was one year old!"

Tiberius responded gravely, "I remember."

"You were ten!"

"But I already loved you. I watched you grow more beautiful every day. You were my delight, you made it all worthwhile."

Vipsania reflected. "You were always so polite to me, so gentle; you made me feel… grown-up. The other children teased me, but I liked it."

She produced a ring with a shining blue stone, exquisitely engraved with a portrait of Venus. Tiberius was amazed.

Vipsania explained: "I do not remember the occasion, but I do remember the date. Venus because… I believe she loves us."

He put the ring on his finger and gazed at her. Gradually, his smile

faded into an anxious frown. Vipsania tilted her head, asking why.

"It worries me, Vipsania. I am so happy. The gods envy such happiness. They take it away."

Vipsania pretended to misunderstand him. "Yes, the cucumbers have been very good this year. We shouldn't take them for granted."

Tiberius persisted. "The stars say that I will have power and wealth, but not love. And I have all three."

Vipsania stroked his brow and pulled closer. They embraced as Tiberius lifted his eyes to the portico ceiling. It had been painted with stars and planets in the positions they held on the November night of his birth. He believed in their tyranny; he felt himself impaled by them, like so many bolts, onto the framework of his life. He wished he could read them, to know when his sorrows would come.

Chapter 3 - The Gods Intervene

A few nights later, Augustus' daughter Julia was entertaining a guest at her villa in Rome. A small woman, Julia had flashy looks and gestures, and bright captivating eyes like her father's. She was only 26, with dark brown hair that was already turning gray. She augmented her charms by draping herself in the most elegant clothing and the most exquisite jewelry in Rome. Julia had intelligence, a restless energy, and an unlimited capacity for enjoyment – she was irrepressible.

The bedroom was decorated with the finest curtains, sculptures, and paintings. Bronze lamps and tripods sputtered and plumed with smoke. Musicians in the shadows played a soft melody on flutes and stringed cithars, cymbals chiming imperceptibly in time with the music.

In the middle of the room was a large round bed, covered with embroidered cushions and shimmering cloths. The room was a shrine - to love, and to lust - and the bed was its altar, surrounded by life-size bronze statues of nymphs and satyrs, their nude bodies seeming to move in the quavering light. In the center was Julia, writhing in the ecstasies and sufferings of lovemaking with a man named Sempronius Gracchus.

A man and a woman approached them tentatively. The musicians hesitated and then stopped playing.

"My lady!"

Julia rolled onto her back and railed at her maidservant.

"How *dare* you interrupt me! Is the house on fire? The house had *better* be on fire!"

"But my lady... your husband... he has died!" There were gasps from the lover and musicians.

The servant continued: "The Pannonian fever worsened, my lady. He was unable to take food or drink. Marcus Agrippa is dead."

"Was my father with him?"

"No, my lady. Your husband died before Augustus Caesar had reached Campania."

Julia felt a twinge of regret; her father had pressed her to accompany him, but she pleaded pregnancy and stayed behind. She pulled a thin wrap over her breasts, shuddered slightly, and stepped out of bed. She circled it slowly - no tears, but she was moved and a bit confused, thinking what this meant to her.

Marcus Agrippa was 51, her father's age and almost his equal in status and power. She didn't love him, but they had four children and she was expecting a fifth. Their futures depended on her husband's position. Now that Agrippa was gone, she had to attach herself to his replacement.

So her mind was moving already.

Sempronius Gracchus spoke: "Your husband was a great man, Julia.

The greatest man, after Augustus. He will be missed."

Julia ignored him, then suddenly started from her thoughts and dismissed him: "You may go, Gracchus... I will be in touch..."

There was a pause. She continued absentmindedly: "Probably..."

Agrippa's passing was marked by an extravagant display of public mourning. A swelling throng of the bereaved followed his body as it was carried north from Campania to Rome, a distance of 100 miles.

He was the favorite of the people at large, both for his humble origins and for his improvements to Rome and other cities, most of them benefiting the common people especially. He built aqueducts and hundreds of fountains, and he opened free baths for unrestricted public use. Open squares, parks, and buildings had been planned and paid for by the great benefactor.

It was Marcus Agrippa who delivered the "bread and circuses" that kept the Roman people happy and made Augustus' position secure. As a parting gift, Agrippa left every Roman citizen a gift of 400 sesterces, roughly a year's pay for a common laborer.

Agrippa's body was carried by a group of senators to the *Campus Martius* (Field of Mars), where it was cremated. The ashes were taken by the leading Roman knights and placed in the mausoleum built by Augustus for himself and his family.

After the ceremonies, several members of the imperial family gathered in the *atrium* of Tiberius' home. He sat on the edge of the *impluvium*, the square pool beneath a skylight in the middle of the room, his arm around Vipsania's shoulder. She ached with the death of her father, outwardly calm but disoriented, her eyes reddened by a week of tears. She squeezed her husband's hand repeatedly.

The women wore the white of mourning; the men were in black. At Vipsania's side was her mother Attica, whom Agrippa had divorced when Vipsania was five so he could marry Augustus' niece. Livia was also present, and Tiberius' brother Drusus with his wife Antonia and their three year-old son, later to be known as Germanicus. He and Vipsania's little Drusus played with a young servant in a corner of the room.

Livia clearly presided over the group; all eyes were on her, watching for a clue. What would happen next? When she didn't speak, Tiberius broke the silence: "There has never been a more magnificent funeral in all of Roman history. Appropriate for such a great and good man."

Attica followed: "Yes, even though he divorced me, we remained friends. And he was always a good father to Vipsania."

Tiberius continued: "He taught me much - he was irreplaceable."

Drusus responded: "But he *will* be replaced, Tiberius, and soon. Augustus believes that the only way to avoid civil war when he dies is for an established heir to take his place. *You* are the logical choice."

Attica was surprised. "Tiberius? But what about Julia and her sons? We know how important that is to him. 'The line of the divine Julius Caesar' and all that. Surely Julia will have a say?"

Livia intoned diplomatically, "Augustus has great hopes for his grandsons. But they are only boys, Attica. Gaius is just eight, Lucius five. Tiberius is the logical choice to replace Agrippa until Gaius and Lucius are ready. He might even marry Julia to a lesser man, to avoid complicating the succession."

Drusus and Tiberius glanced at each other. Drusus said, "I don't see Julia settling for a nonentity she's been wife and mother to Augustus' heirs. She won't settle for less!"

There was a pause while everyone groped for a solution. Only Livia could think of one. She tried to change the subject. "Enough of this! Today we remember Agrippa."

Antonia still had Julia on her mind. She whispered to Attica as they strolled to the courtyard: "She didn't even go to his deathbed!"

Attica replied, "She *is* pregnant, my dear."

"Pregnancy hasn't interfered with her social life!" observed Antonia. "They say she was with Sempronius Gracchus when she heard the news!"

Attica nodded. "Yes, her infidelities always worried Marcus. If his paternity was doubted, it could affect their children's futures, But Julia is no fool – she is always careful."

Antonia smiled at this. "Yes, I know. How did she put it? 'I never take on passengers unless I have cargo on board.'"

Chapter 4 - The Wheels Turn

The next afternoon, Julia was with Augustus at his home. The emperor was clearly grieved by the death of his old friend, son-in-law, and colleague.

Augustus was 50, somewhat small in stature, but trim and with a spring in his step. There was something fragile about him – his wrists and neck were thin, his cheeks a trifle hollow. He had bright, penetrating eyes, and curly blond hair, giving way to white around his ears. Despite his ruthlessness in politics, he had an easy, friendly manner.

Julia looked away from her father during their conversation, to hide her expressions.

"Father, the daughter of the emperor cannot remain single. I'll need a new husband."

Exasperated, Augustus replied, "You've only just buried your old one, Julia! You must wait a year – or ten months at least. And the choice is an important one."

She wasn't listening. She went on, half to herself, somewhat aroused by the thought, "Tiberius, I think..."

Unknown to Augustus, Julia had tried several times to seduce Tiberius. Her failure had only increased her passion for him.

Augustus' jaw dropped: "Tiberius!? But he's married to Vipsania, your late husband's daughter! They have a family!"

Julia replied, impatiently, "And he is the best man, the *only* man, to fill Agrippa's shoes!"

Augustus tried to divert her: "Actually, I was thinking of marrying you to a man of no distinction this time. Someone who wouldn't interfere with my plans for Gaius and Lucius."

Julia was aghast. "And have my children, descendants of the divine Julius Caesar, in the house of *a nobody?* Who will protect them when you are gone?"

There was a pause, she lowered her voice. "Father, don't you see? My children are too young to rule. If anything should happen to you, power

will go to the most capable man. But will he tolerate the grandsons of Augustus as his rivals? No! He will kill them - and me."

Augustus could not argue with this – it had crossed his mind. It was why he had married Julia to Marcus Agrippa - so that Agrippa would not envy her sons when she had them.

"But if I am *married* to the most capable man in Rome, then how can he kill us? My sons will be his sons, and eventually his heirs. Tiberius is your stepson and the most capable man in Rome; he *must* be my husband. There is no other way."

Augustus knew she was right, but he said nothing. Livia entered the room and took Augustus' arm. He said to her:

"She wants to marry your son, Tiberius."

Livia struggled to hide her elation. The very solution she had imagined before, but she waited to respond, as if turning a new idea over in her mind.

"Tiberius? Hmmm. Yes, it makes sense. Of course! I agree! The perfect match!"

Julia was pleased with herself. So was Livia; this would assure her son's position as Augustus' right hand man and heir - for the time being, at least.

———

The following day, Tiberius was summoned by Augustus. As he approached the reception chamber, he passed Julia going the other way. He took her hand. "My deepest condolences, dear Julia. If there is anything I can do..."

She assumed a pious expression, "Thank you, Tiberius," but then she flashed a wicked, slightly seductive smile at him, "there will be."

Nonplussed, he watched as she hurried down the corridor.

As he entered the room, Livia moved to greet him. Augustus arose from his chair and asked: "How is Vipsania?"

"Quite upset, naturally."

The emperor replied, softly: "Of course. I am sure that Attica will see her through."

"Yes, her mother is very supportive, but she relies on me especially. She was her father's daughter."

"Yes, I know. He was very fond of her." Augustus motioned for the servants to leave.

"Tiberius, we must talk of the future. I know that, in the long view, you disapprove of the principate. But you do see that it was the only way to end the civil wars?"

Tiberius was surprised that Augustus wanted to talk politics.

"Yes, I see that. You ended a century of political chaos and bloodshed. But sir, the senate and the noble families must have a role in government. Our goal must be to return power to their hands now that the crisis has passed."

"Have I not shown the utmost respect to the senate, to the noble families?"

Tiberius responded cautiously. "Of course! But sir, the senators are forgetting how to govern. The important decisions are taken by you and your advisors. Senate meetings are just empty show these days. The senators have no real responsibility, no power - only the appearance of it."

"Tiberius, the senate is full of wolves and vultures, as it has been for more than a century. Do you realize what will happen if I am not succeeded by a competent man? The civil wars will return. Chaos will reign and Rome's enemies will pick her bones."

"I accept that. I am a republican, but I am also a realist. The senate is in no position to rule. Your position must be unassailable."

Augustus turned towards him, "And that is why I must have a colleague, ready to carry on should I die. As long as Agrippa was alive, I knew that the peace and stability of the empire would survive my passing. But now? I must raise a man to Agrippa's position immediately. Otherwise, we will have achieved nothing but a pause in a century of violence."

Tiberius nodded slowly in agreement. He knew that he was the only man with the experience and family connections to fill the role. He did not want it, but he had to do what Augustus was on the point of asking him to do.

"Do you understand what I am saying, Tiberius?" Tiberius thought he did. He did not.

"You must divorce Vipsania and marry Julia. It is the only way to consolidate the family's position, your position. Your wife's political usefulness died with her father. Julia is your future now."

Tiberius felt the words strike him. He actually stumbled. "But I love Vipsania, more than my own life!"

"Do you love her more than your country?"

There was an awkward pause. Augustus was uncomfortable demanding this, but he didn't feel he should have to explain further. He expected Tiberius to understand; it was a matter of duty.

"I am not making a suggestion, Tiberius, this is an order. You *will* marry my daughter. The betrothal must take place as soon as possible, so there is no doubt about my arrangements for the future. Do you agree?"

In a softer tone: "Tiberius, you are a member of the Claudian clan. You know that duty to Rome comes first for a man in your position. Look at the sacrifices your father made for his duty – even releasing your mother."

Tiberius set his jaw in defiance. He towered over Augustus; placed his hands on his hips. But Augustus glared up at him with a menacing look. Augustus was not only his stepfather, he had been consul eleven times, he had the power of a tribune, he was the *Pontifex Maximus* - high priest of the state religion - and imperator of the Roman armies. All of these were qualifications that Tiberius regarded with deep respect and awe.

Vipsania's face entered his mind. He imagined losing her. He imagined telling her. He felt nauseous - the contents of his belly squirmed into his mouth. He forced them back and breathed rapidly. No! He would not agree. He would die first.

"No! I will not do it. If you insist upon it, there is an honorable alternative."

Augustus was appalled: "You would kill yourself to avoid marrying my daughter?"

"No – to avoid living without the woman I love!"

Livia intervened, speaking softly to Augustus, "He loves her. You know his attachments are strong. Let me speak with him."

Augustus stormed out – pausing to point a meaningful finger at Tiberius.

Livia rushed to Tiberius and slapped him hard on the left cheek! And again! Tears spilled from his eyes.

In her loudest possible whisper, she hissed: *"Tiberius!* Think! What will happen to us if Julia marries someone else? Do you think another man will tolerate a rival like you?"

"But Vipsania is my life."

"Don't you think I was attached to your father? And yet I left him for Augustus. Why? Because it was my duty - to my country and to my children. If I had refused, would you be in this position today?"

Tiberius gave her an ironic look.

She was exasperated. "You must understand, Tiberius, you have no choice in the matter. It has been decided. If you refuse, you will lose Vipsania anyway, and your entire family will suffer. Marry Julia or lose everything."

Chapter 5 – The Price of Power

Tiberius struggled home. It was an effort to walk – he had to stop several times to catch his breath. Vipsania greeted him at the door and they strode arm in arm to the courtyard. She knew that something was terribly wrong.

"What did Augustus say? Must you return to the army so soon? Is there a crisis? Tiberius, what has happened?"

He looked into her eyes, knowing that the words he was about to utter would change their lives forever.

"He wants me to marry Julia. Divorce you and marry Julia." She neither moved nor breathed.

"I told him no, but he won't accept it."

He was alarmed by her reaction. She turned pale and said nothing. As soon as the words had escaped his lips, Vipsania knew her future. Like her mother, she would lose her husband to politics. She felt a sharp, throbbing, growing pain in her upper belly. It seemed that if she spoke or moved, something terrible would happen.

Tiberius was horrified. He tried to help her to a stool, but she collapsed at his touch. The servants, watching from the shadows, hurried to help.

Three days later, Tiberius had not eaten nor left Vipsania's bedside. She had lost the baby. The house had echoed with screams and moans for three days.

Vipsania woke just before dawn; she heard a dove in the distance; surveyed the dimly lit room – then realized that Tiberius was holding her hand. She was tired and numb, but she was finally able to think.

Few of the marriages she knew were based on affection. It was politics and business that chose husbands and wives. Power was Tiberius' destiny

– all of his life had prepared him for it. Rome needed him more than they needed each other.

Perhaps it was a kindness that it should happen now, when she had just lost her father. There was a limit to how much pain a person could feel, and she had certainly reached it. She had to make it as easy for him as possible.

Tiberius raised his head. "How are you, my love? Is there pain? Can I do anything?"

"I'm just tired, so tired."

"This is my fault. I should never have wavered. My weakness has cost us our child. I will die before I leave you, Vipsania. When you are strong enough, we will escape, leave the empire."

Vipsania knew better. Her heart was aching, but she was too weak to cry. She had to let fatigue make her seem calm and resigned.

"No, Tiberius, we must obey. This is the price of our position, my love. We understand this. Your mother left your father. My father left my mother. And now my father's death has changed everything. We always knew this could happen. We will survive. For little Drusus, we must survive. Think of the future he has been born for – would you make him an exile before he has his teeth?"

Tiberius kissed her hand, grateful that she was stronger and wiser than he. They were quiet together, watching the sunlight spread across the room. The servants began to stir, and the dogs and roosters in the distance. Finally, Vipsania broke the spell.

"Why couldn't we be obscure, Tiberius? Why couldn't we be simple shepherds in some remote province, or German tribesmen in a dark forest, far from the call of duty? Then we could always be together."

Tiberius looked at her, set his jaw, "I want you to know. No matter what we do. In my heart, you will always be my wife."

Vipsania turned away from him. "That will be an easier fiction for you than for me, Tiberius. Julia is an independent sort of woman, and you will be with the army most of the time. But I will be married to a man not of my choosing. I will have to bear his children, and his manners."

"And what will become of Drusus?"

Vipsania lost control. Her voice became high and thin, broken by her sobs. "He will live with you and Julia, of course! Augustus will have plans for him. It is all 'for the good of Rome.'"

She struggled to compose herself. Tiberius covered his face with both hands.

Later that day, Vipsania strengthened a little. She was able to eat.

Tiberius reported to Augustus.

"Well?"

"Vipsania is a better Roman than I am. I will do as you say."

"Good! You must divorce immediately so that the betrothal can take place. The wedding will be early next year, after the necessary period of mourning. But Tiberius, you must prepare to leave at once for Pannonia. The rebellion has flared up again. The barbarians were cowed by Agrippa, but now that he is gone, they have found their courage."

Tiberius was dismayed: "But Vipsania is still very weak. You know she lost the baby. I…"

Augustus gripped his shoulder. "She has her mother, Tiberius. She is not your concern anymore. This affair in Pannonia is serious; it requires your full attention. Besides, the change will be easier for you this way. Best to leave Rome and be busy."

Chapter 6 -More Wheels

Others were aware of the ramifications of Agrippa's death. Gaius Asinius Pollio, one of the most ambitious and politically astute members of the senate, realized that Vipsania would soon be cast adrift by Tiberius, who had to marry Julia or be superseded by a lesser man.

Pollio was bald and lean. At 64, he had lost none of the insight and flexibility that had enabled him to survive the careers of Pompey the Great, Julius Caesar, Mark Antony, and then Augustus. One of the most brilliant Romans alive, he was the author of numerous books, including histories, critical essays, and tragic poems. He established the first public library in Rome and had been the friend of Horace, Vergil, and Catullus.

He also had had a distinguished public career, always knowing when to switch sides or disappear from view. And now he could see a chance to improve his family's position.

His son Gaius Asinius Gallus was only thirty, but his father's equal in ambition, arrogance, and opportunism. Like Pollio, he was short and wiry, with darting eyes and a small upward sloping nose that always put Tiberius in mind of a rat, sniffing around for a piece of cheese. The two young men, different in so many ways, had disliked each other since early childhood. Gallus was quicker than Tiberius, but less profound and with fewer scruples. They were the mongoose and the cobra.

Augustus had observed more than once that Gallus would like to be an emperor. But he considered him to be disqualified for rule by the narrowness of his ambition – putting his personal and family welfare above that of the state.

"He thinks he follows me in this," said Augustus, "but I put my family first for *the good of the state!"*

Pollio and Gallus reclined for dinner with a few guests – a customarily sumptuous affair. The food was served on solid gold plates on a table made from a single slab of wood more than six feet across. The table alone cost a million sesterces, enough to make a man wealthy.

Pollio spoke excitedly as he dismembered a lobster. "Think of it, Gaius. Your sons would be the half-brothers of Drusus, Livia's grandson. They would mingle with the imperial family, perhaps even marry into it. This is too good an opportunity to miss. And who else will dare to marry Vipsania? Tiberius will be furious."

Gallus grinned mischievously.

Pollio continued: "And remember, Vipsania is the granddaughter of Atticus – the richest man in Rome in my day. Her dowry will no doubt be returned to her; a tidy sum I am sure."

A dinner guest, looking at Gallus, added: "She isn't bad looking either."

Gallus was dismissive, "Not my type, but that isn't important. I'll still have my mistresses and slaves. We know she is fertile – Drusus is a strapping lad – though this miscarriage concerns me."

Pollio waved it off, "It was shock, that's all. Losing her father and divorced so suddenly. She is young; she will recover."

He scanned the room for further comments. No one had any. He clapped his hands together. "Good! But we must act quickly, before Augustus makes his own choice. We will see him tomorrow, before Tiberius leaves for Pannonia."

Gallus frowned. "Is that wise? As you say, Tiberius will be furious." "Yes, but Augustus will not commit Vipsania to anyone while Tiberius is away. He'll want his approval."

Chapter 7 - The Deed is Done

The divorce proceedings were held in Vipsania's room where she lay in bed, still recovering from her miscarriage. Livia, Attica, a few servants, the famous doctor Musa, a pair of magistrates, and a scribe were all present.

The scribe handed a document to the senior magistrate, who read aloud. Tiberius stood beside the bed, both hands clasping one of Vipsania's. The tears streamed down their cheeks as the terms were pronounced:

"To Caesar Augustus, guardian of the parties mentioned herein, being Tiberius Claudius Nero, son of Livia, stepson of the addressee, and Vipsania Agrippina, step granddaughter and daughter in law of the addressee, to wit: That the union of the aforementioned parties is hereby dissolved, that the parties declare their intention to remain apart and that it shall be lawful for either party to enter into marriage with another party. That the dowry provided for Vipsania Agrippina by her father, Marcus Vipsanius Agrippa, described in detail in the attached documents, shall be restored to her by the wish and consent of Tiberius Claudius Nero. That the issue of the marriage to be dissolved, namely Nero Claudius Drusus (little Drusus), shall remain in the household of his father, that the servants belonging to each party at the time of the marriage shall revert to the original separate households. That the servants acquired since the time of marriage shall…"

Tiberius and Vipsania didn't hear a single word. They stared into blankness, like captives in war, knowing they would be executed or sold into slavery. It was the worst moment of their lives.

The next morning, after the betrothal ceremony - almost as painful for him as the divorce - Tiberius entered Augustus' reception chamber. He was in uniform, ready to leave for Pannonia. Pollio and Gallus were with the emperor. Tiberius nodded, but he was not happy to see them. On the other hand, their presence made it easier for him to hide his anger with Augustus.

The emperor turned to greet him. "Ah! Tiberius. Ready to march, I see. Perhaps we can settle one more piece of business before you leave. Gallus has offered to marry Vipsania. An excellent match for her, don't you think?"

Tiberius felt an impulse to strangle his stepfather. After all, Augustus knew of his contempt for Gallus. But Tiberius quickly realized this was not Augustus' idea. It was Pollio's scheme; a way to insinuate himself into the imperial family.

Like a tower of stones in an earthquake, Tiberius shook but did not fall, slowly gaining control of himself. The three men watched him with dread on their faces, knowing how he must feel and fearing how he might act.

Finally he took a deep breath and spoke to Gallus: "Aren't you concerned by the difference in status?"

Gallus answered breezily. "Yes, of course, but I am willing to overlook her *father's* humble origins, and that her *grandfather* was only a knight."

Tiberius moved towards him, his fists clenched, but Augustus blocked his way, cheerfully scolding the impudent senator. "Now Gallus, you know Vipsania has other connections that will do you no harm whatsoever."

Then, in a low voice to Tiberius as he pulled him aside: "This was not my idea, but can you think of a better family for her to be connected with? Think of Vipsania, Tiberius, and her future children. Her sons will be qualified for the highest offices. Gallus has talent, wealth, position."

Tiberius spat out the words: "And a very high opinion of himself."

Tiberius felt blank; helpless. He knew he had no rational grounds for objection. He did not like Gallus, but Pollio was a great man and his family was sound. Sarcasm was all that was left to him.

Augustus clasped his shoulder and lowered his voice even more, "Yes, but with some justification. There is no better match politically for her. Or for us, come to that. You know how ambitious they are. This will tie them to your son, to our family. Do you see?"

Tiberius grunted and turned to leave. Augustus snorted after him, "Do…you… approve?" Without looking back, Tiberius raised his hand in agreement and left the room.

Chapter 8 – The Storyteller (AD 36)

Forty-seven years later, the heart of Roman power had shifted south to the Isle of Capri off the coast of southern Italy. Home to the aged emperor Tiberius, its jagged landscape teemed with soldiers and politicians. There were flocks of children, disguised as nymphs and satyrs, and the hills crawled with philosophers. There were also envoys from every part of the empire, and beyond.

Among the visitors was Alcinous, a young Greek student who had come from Egypt to study under Thrasyllus, the famous scholar and astrologer who was the emperor's close friend and advisor. Alcinous had heard repulsive things about Capri – and about Tiberius. He wanted to leave as soon as possible - and take his teacher with him.

"Come back to Alexandria," he pleaded. "Finish your days in your own city. You will be the king of philosophers there; the new Plato."

Thrasyllus, a wiry, white-bearded man with pointy black eyebrows and a cane, was not tempted. The boy could not imagine what it meant to be the emperor's confidante and Thrasyllus was too tired to explain.

"There is philosophy here, too, Alcinous. Tiberius has collected all the best minds. There is a symposium nearly every day – it is quite stimulating."

Unimpressed, Alcinous lowered his voice. "Is it because he won't let you leave?"

Thrasyllus bristled: "I am a free man – I go where I want."

Alcinous was silent as he gathered up some scrolls. He hesitated. "May I speak freely?"

Thrasyllus looked around cautiously. "You, too, are a free man – but speak softly."

"People say this is a playground of sensuality, where he indulges his vile passions."

"Could I remain in such a place?"

Alcinous gestured toward a group of boys dressed as satyrs, chasing a stray lamb around a Priapus herm – a statue of a fertility god with a huge erect phallus, which the children were gripping for balance.

Thrasyllus shook his head vigorously. "No, you misunderstand. He enjoys the gaiety; he likes children. His own childhood was brief and uncertain, and his children were taken from him."

Alcinous tried a different approach. "The trials, the executions - many for no apparent reason. Is this the fruit of his philosophy?"

"The reasons are real, though they may not be apparent to you."

"But even his friends have been put to the sword!"

"None that were *truly* his friends. Alcinous. There is much that you don't know about Tiberius; that no one knows. He has suffered mightily, like Ixion on his burning wheel. He, too, is a free man, but less free than you or I to make choices."

The student was amazed. "What is it that an emperor cannot choose?"

"What he wanted most - a simple life; to be a family man. He had that once, but it was taken away. All the power in the world could not bring it back. The measure of a man is how he spends his old age. Look around you, Alcinous - Tiberius creates a paradise and pursues wisdom."

Alcinous was intrigued. Thrasyllus made Tiberius sound almost like Plato's philosopher king. Or perhaps he had tried to make him one, and refused to see that he had failed?

"You met him on Rhodes, isn't that right?"

"Yes, more than thirty-five years ago. Tiberius was like a prisoner there, longing for Rome. He begged Augustus for permission to come home and see his family, but the emperor refused. Tiberius hoped for a change in fortune and consulted many astrologers. That is how we met."

"Why did he go to Rhodes in the first place? They say it was to escape from Julia and her sons, or because he was worn out by the wars."

"Yes, so they say." Thrasyllus smiled.

"There was another reason?"

Thrasyllus walked to the window. "It is a lovely day, shall we walk?"

They moved away from the main villa, which was perched on top of a sea cliff a thousand feet high. As they followed a steep trail that over-looked the water, Thrasyllus wondered if he should tell the whole story. It bothered him that Tiberius was misunderstood by so many. He knew the emperor to be a just and efficient ruler, and, as his advisor, Thrasyllus had a personal stake in his reputation. Alcinous was just the sort of man to confide in – intelligent, discreet; young enough to keep the truth alive.

"Alcinous, you must not repeat what I am about to tell you while Tiberius still lives – or while I still live, at least. He would not thank either of us. But no one will ever understand him without knowing the true story, and I am the only one left who will tell it."

Alcinous shrugged his agreement.

"Keep in mind that I am not a poet nor a storyteller; I am a scholar. My tale may drag in places; my telling of it may not please you. But I guarantee you will never forget it."

Thrasyllus cleared his throat and took a deep breath: "Tiberius went to Rhodes for Vipsania. Everything was for Vipsania."

Astonishment. "Vipsania? His first wife?"

"Even this island, this pastoral pantomime - the sheep, the goats, the satyrs – it's all for her, though she never saw it. It was her fondest wish, to live an idyllic life in the country. This is his homage to her dream."

Alcinous frowned, trying to remember his history, "Why did they divorce?"

"Augustus ordered it."

"But why didn't they remarry, when he became emperor?"

"That is more complicated. But let's not get ahead of the story. To understand Tiberius, you must understand what he has lost."

Chapter 9 - More Battles (11-9 BC)

Thrasyllus described the happiness of Tiberius and Vipsania after their marriage, and the circumstances of their separation. He told Alcinous of Vipsania's betrothal to Gallus, of Tiberius' betrothal to Julia and his journey to the war in Pannonia, so soon after the divorce.

Alcinous was impressed. "Now I understand why he is so bitter."

"No you don't. You have only heard the beginning. What I have told you so far is common knowledge; it is history. It's what people don't know about Tiberius that holds the key to his character.

"His life with Julia was a misery. She was unfaithful, uninhibited, impulsive – everything that he was not. To make matters worse, Tiberius was both envied and congratulated for his misfortunes wherever he went. Every city erected statues of him and Julia together as the 'happy couple.' Of course, he could not betray his true feelings, his longing for Vipsania and his loathing for Julia. Mandatory hypocrisy renewed his wounds and drove them ever deeper.

"Despite their incompatibility, Julia became pregnant within their first year of marriage. With 'fresh cargo' on board, she resumed her sexual adventures while Tiberius was on military campaign. Their son was born in Aquileia, in northern Italy, but he died in infancy.

"Tiberius was furious. He believed that Julia's neglect was responsible for their child's death. He accused her of being callous when she recovered too quickly for his taste - and made this a pretext for breaking off marital relations with her, only two years after the wedding. They remained together officially, but even that charade was soon abandoned."

As Thrasyllus and his student strolled along the path, Alcinous noticed that his teacher was tiring. They took their seats on a marble bench near a statue of Athena holding a spear, her helmet tilted back from her brow and a snake-fringed *aegis* on her breast. Far below them were the harbor, and more cliffs beyond. Distant trumpets announced that Tiberius had begun his rounds.

"Augustus had been right – leaving Rome and going to Pannonia was the best medicine for Tiberius. Warfare was his escape from the subtler battles at home. He loved the straightforward life of the camp, sharing the hardships of the legionary, even his food and routine labors. He has always had an ascetic side, well-suited to life on the frontier.

"As long as Tiberius was away from Rome, he could endure his separation from Vipsania. He could deceive himself that they were only apart for the season, as before. But when he returned to Rome, the reality of his loss would overwhelm him.

"During one of these visits to the capital, a few months after his estrangement from Julia, he attended the dedication ceremony for the *Ara Pacis Augustae* - the Altar of Augustan Peace. It was the thirtieth of January, his mother's 49th birthday."

———

The *Ara Pacis* had been built on the Field of Mars, just a few hundred feet from the mausoleum where Agrippa's ashes were interred three years before. It was erected by the senate in honor of Augustus' successful campaigns in Spain and Gaul, but it celebrated much more than that. It was a monument to his social and religious principles and the lasting peace made possible by his victories.

The altar itself stood in an enclosure that was decorated with painted marble reliefs showing a procession of the imperial family, prominent senators, and other notable Romans. All was dignity and harmony - the golden age of Augustus in stone.

This dedication was a defining moment in Augustus' reign, but its magnificence was lost on Tiberius – he was preoccupied with trying to spot Vipsania among the senators' wives. His roving glance met Livia's – she read his thoughts and glared at him. He glared back.

Vipsania was indeed present. She could see Tiberius, his head poking above the imperial party, so she tried to melt into the crowd. She was afraid of her emotions, should their eyes meet, or if she found herself close to him. She was also afraid of his reaction when he discovered that she was pregnant. Would he see it as betrayal? Sometimes it felt like betrayal, though she knew in her heart it was not. But she couldn't bear to see the hurt in his eyes.

When the senators and their wives filed past the altar - to see the decorations and pay their respects to Augustus and his family - Vipsania held back. Tiberius, certain that she would come forward, moved closer to the enclosure. As he scanned the passing faces, he overheard some children discussing the carved relief on the south side of the monument – the sculptures of the imperial family. They were testing their knowledge:

"Here is Augustus, everyone knows him. And this is Agrippa, but he's dead. And then comes Livia. And this is Tiberius, and the woman looking away from him is Vipsania with her son. They used to be married, but not anymore. Now he is married to Julia, but she's on the other side."

The Greek artists who created these sculptures had had to deal with a sensitive political issue. When they began work, Agrippa was still alive and married to Julia. To accommodate change without offending the memory of Agrippa, they showed Vipsania and Tiberius together in the procession, but looking in opposite directions, to symbolize their separation.

Tiberius studied the monument - his heartbreak had been carved in stone for all to see! What made it worse was that little Drusus was shown with them, holding his mother's hand. But he was shown as he now appeared; a lad of four rather than the infant he had been when his family was last together.

Tiberius left the imperial podium and waded into the crowd. He *had* to find Vipsania! He *had* to see her face. He began to whisper her name – only this kept him in one piece: "Vipsania! Vipsania!"

But there were thousands of people – thousands of faces. He decided to go into the city, to the house of Gallus, and wait for her there. He would be recognized, of course - and what would he do when Gallus saw him? It didn't matter; he *had* to see her!

Vipsania had already left, telling her litter bearers to take her home. She told them to move quickly, but the traffic was against her. Hordes of latecomers were streaming towards them. These people had missed the speeches and rituals, but they did not want to miss the celebration or the public banquet.

The litter was forced to stop. It was very cold. The tears felt like ice on her cheeks. Then she heard his voice: "Vipsania!"

Tiberius had caught up with them. The tears were streaming down his face, but she did not see them - she would not turn around. He hurried after her litter, but she raised her hand. His pace slowed - he understood. He followed when they moved forward, five paces behind, calling her name, all the way to her door.

People stared as they passed – who could miss the distraught prince in his laurel wreath, calling her famous name. Before the next morning, all of Rome knew.

Chapter 10 - Never Again (9-8 BC)

Augustus was livid – even the guards trembled at the force of his words. "How *dare* you insult my family in this way! It is the talk of Rome. What is more, you left your post in the middle of the ceremonies."

Tiberius was calm. "The formalities were over."

"The people came to see us, not just the altar, and you weren't there. The altar celebrates the Roman family – you know how important that is to me, but you left your family so you could chase your *ex-wife!* You undermine my work as well as embarrass me and my daughter – and your mother."

Tiberius stared at nothing, like a soldier being dressed down. Augustus collected himself, assuming the posture of a magistrate.

"You are a member of my household and under my power. If you ever see Vipsania again, if you are ever found in her company, you will pay with your life."

Livia gasped. Augustus turned to her, his finger raised in warning. "I will NOT have my daughter dishonored. Do you understand, Tiberius? You will never see Vipsania again!"

Tiberius lowered his head.

"And don't think you can hide it from me – nothing escapes my notice."

"Nor mine," added Livia, assuring her husband that she supported him.

Augustus continued in a softer tone, "You do Vipsania no favors by approaching her, you know that. Gallus is a jealous, spiteful man. If, as they say, she would not speak with you; that should tell you how she feels. It does her credit."

The morning sun was just peeking over the mainland when Thrasyllus and Alcinous found each other and headed down the path. They said nothing before they reached the statue of Athena, where Alcinous split a loaf of bread between them and waited for the tale to resume.

"After Augustus ordered him never to see Vipsania again, Tiberius fell into an even darker gloom. And the gods sent him new torments. Later that same year, his brother Drusus, his dearest friend and colleague, was thrown by a horse in Germany and died from his wounds. Tiberius traveled 180 miles in a single day to be at his bedside, arriving just in time to see him pass away. Then he walked all the way back to Rome behind the corpse, his grief almost too much to bear.

"His friend Lucilius Longus was with him on the return journey. He told me that one night, as a group of officers sat around a campfire, Tiberius spoke:

"'I can't believe that, after all the hazards of war – the hand to hand combat, even sailing the North Sea – my brother should die from a riding accident.'

"Longus said: 'None of us knows how we will die, Tiberius, or when.' "To which Tiberius replied: 'When I was in Athens with Augustus, I saw an Indian sage leap into a fire - just to show how little his life meant to him. Zarmarus was his name. Longus was there.'

"His friend nodded; there was a pause. Then Tiberius muttered: 'I could do that.'

"Everyone was stunned, at a loss for words.

"Finally, Longus looked meaningfully at Tiberius and said 'But Zarmarus died joyfully.'

"Tiberius understood and said no more.

"After his brother's funeral in Rome, his responsibilities and importance to the state were increased, but it seemed to him that his services were taken for granted. While he was toiling in Germany, Julia entertained an endless stream of lovers. Her friends openly mocked him. They said he was only keeping the seat of power warm until her sons Gaius and Lucius were old enough to occupy it. Increasingly, Tiberius felt exploited by Augustus, forced to do his dirty work, only to be tossed aside in the end.

"As if to add petty irritation to his sorrows, Augustus chose Gallus as one of the two consuls for the year after Drusus' death. You see, Alcinous, Tiberius has always shown the utmost respect to the old republican offices, especially the consulship. Even as emperor, he rises when a consul enters a room and gives way when he meets one of them in the street.

"Gallus knew this and couldn't wait to put Tiberius through his paces. So whenever Tiberius had to visit Rome during the 'Year of Gallus' (in Rome, each year is named for the consuls in office), he employed a scout to make sure their paths never crossed. Meanwhile, Gallus employed one to make certain that they did. In the end, Tiberius' scout was the more nimble. But in the senate house, there was no escape.

"When in Rome, Tiberius made the rounds of banquets and parties, surrounding himself with men who shared his disillusionment and sardonic sense of humor. Among these were two young knights, nobles of the equestrian class, named Vescularius Flaccus and Julius Marinus.

"Marinus was tall, awkward, and none too bright. Flaccus was intelligent and a master of the one liner. The pair of them served as a foil for Tiberius. Wherever he went, all eyes were on him – until Flaccus and Marinus stirred up some hilarity and Tiberius was able to relax on the sidelines.

"Tiberius drank hard and heavily. Flaccus often lampooned his full name - Tiberius Claudius Nero - by calling him 'Biberius Caldius Mero,' which means 'drinker of hot wine without water.' Tiberius' shoulders would quake with laughter at this, but every banquet ended the same way – with a woozy but glum Tiberius regretting his past, shedding tears for Vipsania."

Chapter 11 - Her New Life

As great as Tiberius' troubles may have been, they were small compared to Vipsania's. Her new family, the Asinii, was both proud and ambitious. Its members resented the heights to which her father Agrippa had risen. He was a "new man" and unworthy, in their view, to hold such high offices as consul and tribune and to marry the daughter of Augustus. Also, they had supported Mark Antony, whose defeat was the result of Agrippa's military skill. Now that Agrippa was dead and his eldest daughter under their control, they soothed themselves by torturing her.

Vipsania's husband and father-in-law were largely indifferent to the women of the household, so she fell especially under the power of Salonina, her mother-in-law. She was a small, round woman, with black hair pulled so tightly into a multitude of braids and buns that it seemed to make her eyes bulge.

Salonina ruled the domestic realm with a relentless attention to detail that often threatened Vipsania's sanity. Vipsania's situation scarcely eased when she provided her new family with sons – two since her marriage to Gallus, and a third child was on the way.

Vipsania seldom saw her husband. There was no emotional intimacy between them and their sex life was perfunctory and unsatisfying. Gallus enjoyed various mistresses and slave boys, but Vipsania had only the memory of Tiberius' warmth and tenderness.

Gallus was indifferent to her feelings and condescending toward her tastes and opinions. Vipsania realized this would be so even before the wedding took place. She knew that Pollio was a literary man, a writer, historian, and patron of the arts, and that Gallus followed his father in these tastes. Literature was Vipsania's passion and she hoped that this might form a bridge between them. These hopes were soon dashed.

Pollio raised the subject after the betrothal ceremony.

"So, Vipsania, I understand that you do a little reading. Whom do you admire?"

"Yes, I love to read. My mother encouraged it and kept me well-supplied with books. Among the Greeks, I adore Theocritus and the other pastorals. I read all I can find. Also the classics, of course, and Menander. Tiberius gave me a taste for small doses of Meleager..."

Pollio shook his head impatiently. "Latin authors, please!"

He had made her self-conscious. "I greatly enjoy your works, of course. (She didn't – much too dark for her taste – but she wanted to please him.) And the other great Roman authors of our day, especially the poets."

"Names?"

"Well, Vergil, naturally, especially his Eclogues. And Horace. Catullus. Livy. Lucretius interests me. And Cicero."

Both Pollio and Gallus broke into open laughter. The others present, including Salonina, snickered to themselves.

Pollio patronized her, *"Cicero?* My dear, haven't you read my criticisms? It is now accepted that he was a mediocrity. Sand without lime."

Gallus chimed in, "And enough sand to dam the Tiber!" There was dismissive laughter all around.

Pollio moved on, "No, Cicero is not to be admired. His speeches were occasionally useful, but we do not take his writings seriously."

There was an element of finality and even warning in the last remark that brought tears to Vipsania's eyes. She struggled to hide them, hoping they would dry before they rolled down her cheeks. She cherished Cicero. He was her grandfather's closest friend, her mother's favorite. Pollio and Gallus knew this. She knew they knew this.

Vipsania was tormented by another imperious woman besides her mother-in-law. Julia, who resented her possession of Tiberius' heart, controlled access to her son Drusus. Getting permission from Salonina to visit Drusus was almost as difficult as obtaining permission from Julia to see him when she did. Many times, she was turned away from Julia's door because "something has come up" or because Drusus was "unwell."

To intensify her pain, her son grew more distant with each meeting. He resented the infrequency of her visits and was too young to understand the reasons why.

She worried about her son. She did not approve of how Julia dressed him, in short tunics with his hair curled and his cheeks rouged. She was afraid that he would be used by his stepmother's friends, some of whom were actors, gladiators, soldiers - rough men, and with his father away most of the time.

But Vipsania had no more influence where Drusus was concerned than with her boys at home. It had been clear from the start that her children would be raised by Salonina. Her role was to produce them, but decisions about their education, friends, and behavior would be made by others in the family.

Vipsania often thought of her mother. She had needed to apply to Agrippa's wives, including Julia, to see Vipsania and she, too, had had no control over how her daughter was raised or treated. Vipsania hadn't realized what a helpless feeling Attica must have had. She now regretted that she was sometimes cruel to her mother, indignant that she had abandoned her. She also had been too young to understand.

Tiberius was often on her mind – especially the altar episode. She dreamt about it, over and over. In her dream, she turned to him, she joined him and they ran away together. The crowd shouted after them, but they kept running. She envied Tiberius his ability to leave Rome. She was a prisoner, despised by her jailors and cut off from those she loved most.

A temporary reprieve from her hardships came a year after Gallus' consulship when he was chosen to serve as governor of the province of Asia, in western Asia Minor. Vipsania would accompany him on this year- long assignment (Agrippa was worshipped in the east and Gallus wanted to display his daughter).

To Vipsania's joy, both Salonina and Pollio would stay behind in Rome. She might even have some freedom while Gallus toured the province, leaving her in a major city with the children. She had always wanted to travel, to this part of the world especially, home of so many of her literary heroes.

Salonina anticipated her daughter-in-law's happiness and tried to make her as uncomfortable as possible: "I guess you're glad to take a holiday while I stay here and run the household as usual. But you had better not revert to your old habits while you're gone, Vipsania, or I will boil you alive when you return. Remember that you will be representing *our* family."

Chapter 12 - A Window Opens (6 BC)

Thrasyllus could tell Alcinous little of Vipsania's trials at this time, but he was well aware of Tiberius' situation. Though he had his differences with Augustus, Tiberius served the state brilliantly. He was rewarded the year after Gallus' consulship with a consulship of his own - his second - and he celebrated a magnificent triumph in Rome for his German victories.

More significantly, he received the power of a tribune for a period of five years. This was a mark of distinction that had only been given to two other men since Augustus took power – the emperor himself and Marcus Agrippa. It set Tiberius apart as the number two man in the empire and heir to the throne.

Tiberius was indeed following in Agrippa's footsteps. Should anything happen to the sickly Augustus, he would be the undoubted successor. His nearest rival, Julia's son Gaius, was only 14 years old. Some people wanted to see the lad elected consul despite his youth, Julia among them, but he was years away from being ready to rule. For now, Tiberius was the only possible heir.

Thrasyllus resumed his story: "Now, when Agrippa had received the power of a tribune, he used his authority to embellish the city of Rome and satisfy the people with new amenities and entertainments. So all eyes were on Tiberius to see how he would win favor with the mob. Of course, Tiberius cared nothing for popularity. So what did he do? He announced that he would restore the Temple of Concordia in Rome in the name of himself and his brother Drusus.

"Can you imagine the reaction to this? The mob had been licking their lips in anticipation of games and banquets and public amusement parks, and Tiberius gives them a refurbished temple!

"Concordia means many things to the Romans – the cooperation between government and people, the peace and accord of the empire and its provinces. But she had special meaning to Tiberius as a symbol of harmony between a man and a woman. Perhaps he hoped that rebuilding this 360 year-old temple would move the goddess to restore Vipsania to him?"

Thrasyllus checked himself. "Well, probably not. Tiberius is not religious in that sense. He believes that, if the gods exist, they are as powerless to alter fate as men and women are. Nevertheless, the temple became a showplace, adorned with magnificent paintings and famous classical Greek sculptures. The edifice itself was rebuilt in the finest marble, lavishly carved and brilliantly colored."

———

While the restoration work was in the planning stages, Tiberius visited Antonia to discuss her role as Drusus' widow in the dedication. He was surprised to see how much her children had grown. Germanicus was now eight, his sister Livilla six, and the awkward but endearing Claudius three. He had been avoiding his brother's family – both because it made him miss Drusus and because it stirred memories of his life before the divorce. To his surprise, it was now a comfort to be with them – to bask in the family feeling. After business was concluded, he agreed to linger and take a meal.

The wine flowed freely and the conversation turned more serious. Antonia said that she still expected her husband to return each fall; that a part of her did not believe he was gone. Tiberius bristled when she told him of Augustus' insistence that she remarry, and of her absolute refusal. "If only I had been as strong as you when it mattered," he muttered.

Tiberius spoke of his father, how his heart had been broken when he was forced to let Livia go. That he was even required to attend her wedding with Augustus. How he turned to drink and died when Tiberius was only nine.

"I remember the look in his eyes when he tried to explain to me what he thought was important in life – his political views, his disgust over the changes in Roman life and morality. He struggled with the feeling that nothing he said to me would sink in, that I was too young and under the spell of my stepfather - that I would never be his son in any meaningful way. His despair was even greater with Drusus, who was younger. But he was wrong. He did make his impression, on both of us."

There was a flash of anger. "I will not end my days alone like him, a victim of politics."

Tiberius drank deeply. "Antonia, I miss her so much. How is she?"

Antonia wanted to lighten the mood. She had remained close to Vipsania and knew of her unhappiness, which she hid from Tiberius at Vipsania's request. She did not want him to worry about her, or try to intervene, as he probably would. So Antonia spoke only about Vipsania's happiness with her children, of her visits with Drusus, of her excitement over the upcoming trip to Asia.

Tiberius swung his legs off the dining couch and sat upright. "What? She is going with him?"

"Of course. Does that surprise you?"

"No, I suppose not. It's just that – I always think of her as being here in Rome, when I'm away; near Drusus. And, even though I never see her..."

Tiberius' thoughts were racing. Why did this change everything?

———

The sounds of distant pan-pipes startled Thrasyllus from his storytelling. "It is time to dine with the emperor, Alcinous. You will meet him at last!"

Chapter 13 - Banquet (AD 36)

In the center of the dining room was a large round wooden table, which servants kept covered with a succession of fine foods and drink. Seafood was in abundant supply – crabs and mullet were today's featured delicacies, served with a fabulous array of sauces, cheeses, vegetables, sweets, and, of course, cucumbers. A day never passed without cucumbers.

The emperor grew his own cucumbers on Capri in wheeled planting beds that were moved with the sun and covered with panes of transparent mica in winter to protect them from the cold. He inspected them daily and made it clear that cucumber welfare was among his highest priorities.

Tiberius was bald with a white fringe of unruly hair. His long frame was bent over, the pale skin of his face and neck were blotched with red. Alcinous noticed that he wore a ring with a blue stone – the one Vipsania gave him, no doubt. He had the nervous habit of rotating it on his finger while listening to others speak.

Around the table were couches for 30 guests, mostly bearded Greeks: philosophers, writers, scientists, grammarians - plus a few diplomats and princes from distant parts of the empire. Thrasyllus reclined at the emperor's left, with Alcinous beside him. On Tiberius' right was his grand-nephew Caligula, aged 24.

The emperor was dressed and fed like anybody else at the table, but the conversation (in Greek, to Alcinous' relief) belonged to him:

"Before too much wine has flowed into your bellies, I resume my questions."

There were mock groans all around.

"As usual, the prizes will be praise for the winners and contempt for the losers.

"First question: By what name was Achilles known when he hid among the women on Scyros."

Thrasyllus shook his head and said, "Only Thetis (Achilles' mother) would care about that!"

Tiberius admonished him, "Yes, I know you have heard this one before, my old friend. So anyone may answer except Thrasyllus."

There were no takers. The emperor turned to his heir apparent: "Caligula, you have spent enough time hiding among the women. What was his name?"

Caligula was used to this – and good at it. "There are three opinions on the subject. Some say his name was 'Pyrrha,' from which his son Pyrrhus derived his name; others that he was called 'Cercysera' and still others 'Aissa.' But I say he was called Achilles, because he was fooling no one, least of all Deidameia (his girlfriend). Odysseus exposed him with the weapons he brought – but Deidameia had exposed Achilles' weapon long before that."

There was much learned laughter – a combination of bawdy humor and esoteric knowledge was always to Tiberius' taste, as Caligula knew well.

"Very good – worthy of a prince!" said the emperor. "Next question: "Who was the mother of Hecuba, mother of Hector?"

Thrasyllus leaned over to Alcinous and said in a low voice. "Notice that all the questions are about Homer and the Trojan War. You will understand later."

Alcinous nearly choked on his wine when Tiberius called on him. "Young Alcinous, you have been wasting so much of Thrasyllus' time. Surely you have something to show for it?"

Alcinous was not about to be outdone by a mere Roman like Caligula when the subject was Greek mythology.

"Again, Caesar, there are many opinions. Some believe that Hecuba was the daughter of Cisseus, King of Thrace, which would make her mother a Thracian. Others that her father was Dymas, King of Phrygia, so her mother was a Phrygian. However, if she transformed into a dog after the fall of Troy, as is often claimed, then her parentage must have been divine. Therefore I accept the view that her father was the river god Sangarius and her mother Metope, a nymph of the freshwater spring of Arcadian Stymphalos."

"Very impressive, for a Greek," laughed Tiberius. "And now the final question: What songs did the sirens sing that drove Odysseus to distraction?" He called on an elderly mathematician, knowing he would have no idea.

The man stammered. To increase his discomfort, Tiberius warned him,

"Keep in mind that Alexander the Great once said he would execute any scholar who gave him an incorrect answer. However, I am a milder man than Alexander was – I'll only shave your beard."

Finally the man took a guess: "Perhaps ... Alcman's *Hymn to Aphrodite?*"

Tiberius was delighted. "Which was written more than 500 years *after* Odysseus sailed the 'wine-dark sea!'" He lifted his glass and motioned to the guards. "Take him away! Off with his beard!" The poor man was hauled away to thunderous laughter and applause, but only the tips of his long whiskers were clipped, to his obvious relief.

Then the evening grew more serious – readings of poetry, somber musical performance, a set piece of philosophical discussion on a subject chosen by Tiberius: "Why perform good deeds if destiny is predetermined?"

By now, Alcinous was too drunk to comprehend anything.

Chapter 14 - Why Did You Resign? (6 BC)

The next morning, Thrasyllus was more spry than usual, but Alcinous was struggling: too much wine and rich food - and too much Tiberius. He began to understand why Thrasyllus was not tempted to leave this place – there was more going on here than spending taxes.

They strolled to Athena's shrine and Thrasyllus picked up the story. It took Alcinous a moment to remember where they left it – oh yes, Tiberius had learned that Vipsania was going to Asia with Gallus.

The day after his visit with Antonia, Tiberius visited Augustus, wearing a simple tunic rather than a toga or uniform, which surprised Augustus.

"Sir, I wish to take an indefinite leave of absence from my duties, effective immediately."

Augustus was dumbstruck. He pretended not to understand. "Which duties do you mean?"

"My duties as a soldier, as a magistrate, as a diplomat."

Augustus was outraged. "As a Roman, you mean?"

Tiberius didn't flinch. "I am worn out, sir. I have served Rome for 20 years."

"And what do you propose to do instead of serving Rome?"

"I will go to the island of Rhodes and resume my studies. My teacher, the rhetorician Theodore of Gadara, is still there – I learned much from him during my last stay on the island. And there is also the school of the stoic Posidonius."

Augustus couldn't believe his ears. "Socrates said that philosophy should be set aside when a man grows up."

Tiberius answered firmly, "It is because Socrates ignored his own advice that we remember him."

Augustus was exasperated. "I need you here to help me rule. Now that your brother Drusus is gone, you are the only one I can rely upon. No! It is entirely out of the question; you would be deserting your post. It would be nothing less than treason!"

Tiberius was unmoved. "A man's first duty is to his own conscience - the *real* treason is to ignore it. I have rebelled against my conscience for the sake of Rome long enough."

Augustus turned his back on him.

Tiberius continued. "I will do this, sir. I will not eat until you grant my request. If you do not let me go, then I will die and my death will be on your hands."

He left the room.

Livia had listened with astonishment. She knew her son was determined. She turned to Augustus: "He means what he says, husband. Tiberius is slow to commit himself to a course of action, but when he does, he never backs down."

"Then he will starve!"

Livia hurried after Tiberius in the hall. She cut him off and tried to slap his face, but he caught her hand. He held it gently and explained.

"Mother, I will not be his victim like father was. Since I was a teenager, he has made me kill people, tell lies to them, hurt the ones I love - all for the sake of duty. I am just a pawn in his game, to be cast aside when Julia's boys are grown. I must live while I can – be my own man."

"If you will just be patient..."

"Until Gaius takes my place?"

Livia was desperate. "Tiberius, you have enemies. You will be vulnerable without Augustus' support."

"The senate gave me the power of a tribune for five years. He can't take that away from me. I will be safe as long as I hold that office."

Livia knew that it was futile to argue with him. "What will you do in Rhodes?"

"Many things. Recover."

———

Thrasyllus raised four fingers to emphasize his words: "Tiberius neither ate nor bathed for four days. Finally, Augustus relented. The news spread through the city like an August fire. Could the heir to the Roman Empire really quit his job? Everyone looked at Tiberius as if he was a madman; their heads cocked back, their eyes wide. Julia was pleased, of course – now Augustus had no choice but to hurry her sons into power."

Alcinous was impressed. "I had no idea. I heard that Julia drove him away, or that he and Augustus quarreled about military policy or something. But why did he do it? He could have given up some of his responsibilities, or taken a vacation. Why did he walk away from so much?"

Thrasyllus smiled. "Be patient, my friend, you will know soon enough.

"The hardest part was leaving Drusus, now seven years old. In truth, Tiberius had little to do with his son these days. The boy was thoroughly integrated into Julia's circle of children and friends. Drusus was also close to Antonia and her family, especially Germanicus, who was just a year older, which gave Tiberius some comfort. He could not take Drusus with him on this journey.

"Tiberius' entourage when he left was a small one, considering that he was the second most important man in the world. His old friend Lucilius Longus was the only senator to accompany him. There were a few knights, including the opportunists Vescularius Flaccus and Julius Marinus. They were disappointed to see their horse quit the race, but they reasoned that a retired prince might still be a good bet.

"Also in the party were the obligatory *lictors,* attendants of his office who carried the *fasces* - rods and axes that symbolized his right as a *tribune* to beat or execute anyone he chose. No, Tiberius was not leaving empty-handed, but he intended to live simply and never exercise his power, and he almost never did.

"A small group of his closest friends and family traveled the 10 miles to the port of Ostia to see him off. When he boarded ship, he scarcely looked at their somber faces – his mind was on his destination.

"But it was early in the year for travel by sea, and the weather was against them. Soon after setting sail, the captain was forced to shelter along the Campanian coast, just south of Rome, waiting for favorable winds. At one point, the passengers even went ashore for a few days, staying at a local villa. However, one of the knights picked up a rumor in the local tavern that mortified Tiberius.

"'They say that Augustus has fallen ill and that Tiberius lingers nearby in hopes of claiming the throne.'

"Tiberius immediately stormed out of the villa and boarded ship. He told the captain to set sail at once, high seas or not. They left so suddenly that one of the *lictors* had to swim out and be pulled on board.

"Longus was alarmed: 'Tiberius, don't take risks for the sake of rumors. The wind will lighten soon enough.' But Tiberius was determined."

Chapter 15 - Odyssey

The first leg of the voyage was treacherous, with heavy seas and adverse winds. The crew tensed further when they approached the straits of Scylla and Charybdis, between Sicily and the toe of Italy - a dangerous passage at any time of year. The sailors believed it was cursed by the gods. Even Ulysses had lost six men to its fury.

As if on cue, a squall came up when they were committed to the narrows. Foam and spray lashed and tossed the reeling ship, soaking all aboard her to the bone.

Everyone was terrified except for Tiberius, who grinned from ear to ear and laughed out loud as the waves threw him from railing to railing. Longus screamed at him, "Have you gone mad?"

Tiberius shouted back "The greater the danger, the greater the glory. Don't be afraid, my friend; the stars will protect us. And, if not, there are worse fates than death."

Tiberius continued with a theatrical flourish: "I have escaped the cave of the Cyclops! Nor storms nor monsters nor sirens nor kings can keep Ulysses from his Penelope."

Longus was bewildered for a long moment. Then he understood. "You can't be serious! Vipsania is married! She is with her new husband!"

Tiberius turned and smiled at him. "And soon with her old one!"

The storm continued, but the ship held together, and sailing was clear from that point on. Even the captain acquired Tiberius' good cheer when they arrived in the warm and gentle waters of the Aegean.

They stopped at the island of Paros to take on supplies for the last leg of the journey. Tiberius toured the island for a few days, going to see the temples and sculptures made of the famous Parian marble.

Tiberius left Rome in great haste because he feared that Augustus would change his mind and force him to stay. This meant that there had been no time for the rituals that a Roman observes before beginning a journey.

Though Tiberius was not religious in the usual sense, he was Roman to the marrow. It bothered him that he had not made the sacrifice to Vesta that is traditional when one takes up a new post or resigns an old one. So he now went to the Parian temple of Hestia, the Greek Vesta, to make his offering. He climbed the temple steps - and became transfixed when he saw the statue of the goddess.

Tiberius had Vipsania very much on his mind – every young woman looked like her, every sound or scene of beauty reminded him of her. So now he saw her likeness in the statue. The luminous marble reminded him of her soft limbs, the hair was painted her color, and the eyes. The modest turn of the head was so like her. The statue even seemed to move slightly towards him as he approached. The hairs on Tiberius' arms and neck stood on end.

"I must have this statue!" Tiberius proclaimed, looking for someone to hear him. "It must be placed in the Temple of Concordia in Rome as a tribute to... to Vesta."

An elderly priest moved into view, shaking his head. "No, my lord, this is not possible. It would be a sacrilege."

"I will pay you a king's ransom for it."

"But she is not for sale. She belongs to all Parians."

It occurred to the priest that Tiberius could take whatever he wanted. He tried to reason with him. "My lord, Hestia will not be pleased if her statue is removed from this sacred place. It would not be auspicious."

Tiberius was not afraid of the gods. He glared at the priest and said, "I have the power to claim this sacred image for the Roman people – you will be well compensated."

The priest didn't back down. "There will be opposition; a great scandal. There will be consequences."

Tiberius was angry at the threat, but then Flaccus intervened: "My friend and I (indicating Marinus) will pay you 500,000 drachmas for this statue and will commission a new, even finer statue for the same amount. In addition, we will endow the temple with 100,000 drachmas and pay for all the necessary ceremonies and sacrifices to ensure that Hestia is not offended. We will arrange transportation to Rome for this statue in the finest ship available."

Marinus tugged desperately at his tunic, but Flaccus slapped his hand away and whispered in his ear: "Trust me!"

Tiberius remonstrated, "I cannot allow you to do this, my friends." "But we insist," said Flaccus, with Marinus nodding halfheartedly in agreement. "Allow us the honor of doing this for you."

Of course, Flaccus knew that Tiberius would never give in; it would not do for a Claudian to be indebted to a pair of knights. But this only made Flaccus more extravagant in his insistence, until he relented with a flourish of disappointment.

As the priest realized that the argument was no longer about whether the statue would go to Rome but who would pay for it, he reflected on what 600,000 drachmas would mean to the temple, and to himself. He decided to let his objections drop – he would tell the faithful that Hestia gave him a sign of her approval.

Chapter 16 - The Island of Rhodes

Rhodes finally came into view. It was already familiar to Tiberius, who had spent some time there 14 years before. His marriage to Vipsania had been imminent at that time, so the beautiful island had its associations with her. There was something about islands that appealed to him – the isolation, the feeling that one controlled one's destiny when one's world was small.

Tiberius knew that his arrival would cause excitement – he hoped that it would subside quickly. His intention was to live unpretentiously, to wear Greek dress and speak Greek as much as possible - and to avoid using his official powers. However, he knew that he would have to submit to the usual clasping of hands and guided tours when he first arrived.

Eurymachos, one of the leading magistrates of the port city of Rhodes, greeted Tiberius as he disembarked. He was relatively young, with a curly black beard and humorless expression. He tried to take Tiberius by the hand wherever he went, as if the Roman was blind or crippled. He offered him the use of his house in town, which it was convenient for Tiberius to accept temporarily.

"Your kindness is appreciated," he said. "However, I have come to Rhodes for rest and study. I will soon be looking for a small country villa, some distance from the city."

Eurymachos did not hesitate, "And I have the perfect place for you, sir. A guest house on my estate, not less than two miles from town. You may take possession as soon as you wish."

But first were the obligatory entertainments and visits to temples and government buildings. Rhodes was not technically part of the Roman Empire. It was a free but utterly dependent island in the midst of a Roman lake – the Mediterranean Sea. Its people were as attuned to Roman politics as any of her subjects, and as thrilled by such a famous visitor.

Tiberius had long experience of official receptions and public appearances, but that had not made him good at dealing with them. He had a tendency to be too formal and artificial in his speech and manners, which often caused misunderstandings.

When he was taken to the Aesclepion, the temple/hospital of the healing god Aesclepios, Tiberius thought it wise to show his concern for the people there, to give the impression that he would be their benefactor. Helping the sick first would, perhaps, be less of an imposition on his time and not resented by the other citizens, who were eager for favors of their own.

When confronted by a crowd of onlookers waiting to see what he would do, Tiberius made an announcement: "It is my hope to interview all of the sick and infirm people of Rhodes in order to ascertain the reason for their maladies and to determine what can be done to lessen their pain and to avoid an increase in their numbers."

He turned to Eurymachos and the other officials and said, "Please make the arrangements as soon as possible."

The officials misunderstood him completely – they took this as a rebuke, as an indication that he was not pleased by what he saw. So the following morning, Tiberius was ushered to the city's agora where every sick and lame person in the city was on display for his inspection, arranged by complaint.

Tiberius was aghast, and embarrassed. He confronted Eurymachos: "What is the meaning of this?"

The magistrate was nonplussed. "You said that you wanted to see the sick?"

"I meant in their homes, you fool, or in the hospital! What a hardship this must have been for some of these people!"

But the deed had been done, so Tiberius worked his way among the patients, distributing coins and apologies.

The ensuing confusion had one advantage - it allowed Tiberius and Longus to escape Eurymachos and the others and look the city over on their own. It was truly a beautiful place, with a graceful harbor and magnificent views of the sea and the distant mountains. They could make out the giant bronze fragments of the fallen Colossus, the statue of the sun god Helios that had stood as one of the "Seven Wonders of the World" before an earthquake brought it crashing down.

Rhodes was an autonomous state, but its businessmen still had to apply to a Roman magistrate for decisions on trade and to resolve disputes with other cities and provinces. The nearest high official was the governor of the province of Asia - none other than Vipsania's husband Gaius Asinius Gallus!

Near the assembly hall, Tiberius instructed Longus to make inquiries of some magistrates who were conversing outside the building. Tiberius took a seat behind a column and listened intently.

Longus asked anyone who might know, "Greetings, friends. I would like to pay my respects to the new Roman governor in Asia. Does anyone know his itinerary?"

A man who had recently returned from the mainland spoke up, "I have just come from Ephesos. The proconsul Gallus is there now, but he will leave this week to begin his tour of the province. First, he will go north to Pergamum, then into the interior, then to Miletus and Halicarnassus late in the year."

One of the other men asked, "Will he come to Rhodes?"

"There are no such plans."

Longus inquired, "Will his family travel with him?"

"No, the lady Vipsania has small children to care for. They will remain in Ephesos."

Tiberius' heart swelled. His timing was perfect!

Chapter 17 - The Plan

Alcinous considered the situation and shook his head. "But how could Tiberius ever leave Rhodes without raising a fuss? His every move must have been watched."

Thrasyllus nodded, "Yes it was a challenge. You and I take it for granted that we may come and go without attracting notice, but it was different for him. Every city had at least one statue of Tiberius on public display. And he was a tall Roman surrounded by Greeks. However, remember that Tiberius was a wily and resourceful general; he would find a way.

"The first thing was to move into the country villa with his entourage. He spoke firmly to Eurymachos: 'My friend, your hospitality will not be forgotten. But now I must ask you to grant me privacy. I am exhausted from my journey and from my labors – I must have time to myself. You do understand?' Eurymachos bowed and assured him that he would not be disturbed. 'This is my land, sir. No one enters or leaves without my knowing.'

"Eurymachos had alerted Tiberius to another problem – how to escape the villa without *his host* knowing about it? The solution was complicated and depended on a miraculous gift that the gods had given Tiberius, as you will see."

——

Vipsania found everything about Asia exhilarating. Advanced culture was deeply rooted in the Greek East, and she reveled in the historical and literary associations that were everywhere. Her husband was preoccupied with his duties, and there was no Salonina or Pollio to torment and ridicule her.

The city of Ephesos, where she took residence, was magnificent – crowded with glorious buildings and works of art. It was also the home of the most famous shrine in the world – the temple of Artemis/Diana.

To her surprise, Vipsania was received with genuine warmth and interest as the daughter of Agrippa and former wife of Tiberius. While Gallus was seen as a potential bestower of favors, she was valued for a past that she was proud of and delighted to remember.

Late in his life, Agrippa had toured the province and lived for two years on the island of Lesbos. In fact, he had been a virtual "eastern emperor" for quite some time. His many friends and admirers now wished to honor him through kindness to his daughter.

Gallus soon took his small army of soldiers and tax collectors on an extended tour of his new domain. Vipsania would not see him for at least five months! She resolved to take full advantage of her freedom – savoring each day as a gift from Artemis herself.

The lovely city charmed her; its peculiar blend of piety and gaiety suited her particularly well. Her two-story house was on the terraced "Mountain of Nightingales," overlooking the Agora and the vast Theater. Not far away in the other direction was the State Market, the administrative center of the city.

Marcus Agrippa had visited here just a few years before, embellishing it at his own expense and granting the city special privileges. In gratitude, the Ephesians planned to dedicate the south gate of the Agora to him, as well as to Augustus, Livia, and Julia. The gate would be paid for by Mithradates, a former slave of Agrippa's, and by a freedman of Augustus' named Mazaeus.

Mithradates, whom Vipsania vaguely remembered from her youth, was anxious to gain her approval for the monument. To win her favor, he gave a public banquet in her honor in the Agora, where she was showered with gifts and hailed as "the new Diana." She met many local dignitaries and their wives on this occasion, including the high priestess of Artemis, named after her goddess, with whom she felt an instant rapport.

Vipsania's feelings were mixed, however, when she was presented with crude silver portraits of Agrippa and Julia. But her uneasiness dissolved when she saw her father's exaggerated frown and Julia's harsh, unattractive features. The party had no idea why she was laughing, but they took it as a sign they had pleased her.

The legendary Artemision, or temple of Artemis, was some distance away from the city. Its physical size and the grandeur of its ceremonies captivated Vipsania. She often went there by carriage in the early morning with her bodyguard and two of her personal attendants. Hours were spent admiring the lavish temple decorations and the numerous statues and shrines in the vicinity. She strolled through the groves of rare and ancient trees that surrounded the temple complex and gazed at the purple hills beyond.

When the flutes and cymbals began to trill, she returned to the temple and watched the ritual dancing of the *melissae,* or priestesses, and the *megabyzoi* - the eunuch priests who dress like women. As the music and dancing soared to a crescendo, the towering cypress doors of the temple mysteriously swung open, revealing the awe-inspiring archaic wooden statue of the goddess herself. By this time, Vipsania would be mesmerized. The throbbing music, the fragrances, the pulsating colors of the dancers' costumes – all transported her into a blissful, trance-like state. This is why she came to the temple almost every day. She would often join the high priestess for a meal after the ceremonies.

Artemis was a large woman with imperious, aquiline features. Her rich robes and dazzling tiara made her seem even more imposing, but she had a warm, unassuming manner and Vipsania found her approachable and sympathetic. They merrily traded stories of life in palace and temple, intrigued by how similar their experiences had been. Eventually, the stories became more personal.

"I saw your reaction to the portraits, Vipsania. That was unfortunate."

"I must learn to hide my feelings better! They were not to know..."

"...that your father's widow stole your husband? Everyone knows that!"

"But not how I feel about it."

"How do you feel about it?"

Vipsania took a moment. "We Romans are taught to put duty to family and country above all else. I was prepared for the sacrifice mentally, but not emotionally. I truly loved Tiberius. I still do."

Another thoughtful moment.

"It would be easier if my new family wasn't so different from my old one. And if there wasn't a statue of Tiberius on every corner."

Artemis returned to Julia. "She was with your father when he came to Ephesos, you know. I met her. A brilliant woman; very quick-witted."

"Oh yes, and beautiful."

"She reminded me of Cleopatra, which is ironic considering Augustus' views on Cleopatra."

"You met Cleopatra?"

"Yes, I was a novice at the time, but I was assigned to her apartments so I had the chance to observe her. Like Julia, she was bright and ambitious, and very amorous. Restless, too. Always pushing ahead."

She laughed. Vipsania raised her brows to ask why.

Artemis explained: "I think that both Cleopatra and Julia resented that the goddess's house was bigger than theirs."

Both women laughed heartily.

Chapter 18 - Out of the Dark

Thrasyllus was describing Tiberius' arrangements to leave Rhodes as if it was a military operation, which, in a way, it was.

"Only Longus knew that this journey involved Vipsania. The others were only told that Tiberius was anxious to travel incognito, to see how the other half lives."

———

As it happened, Marinus, though a few years younger than Tiberius, was very like him in build and general appearance. Tiberius knew that Eurymachos and his servants would be watching the villa, and that they would be less suspicious if they thought they saw him milling about. So he asked Marinus to impersonate him while he was away.

In the courtyard, away from prying eyes, Marinus put on Tiberius' uniform and received his training: "Be sure to pace back and forth – look as bad-tempered as possible. Talk to yourself and throw your arms around. I don't want people to be tempted to visit you. Or me, that is. Now show me."

Marinus was reluctant at first, but then he burst into a greatly exaggerated impersonation, striding rapidly with his head jutting forward, gesticulating with his fingers as he muttered to himself. Everyone laughed, including Tiberius, "I want you to look irritable, not insane!"

One of the *lictors* raised an objection, "Sir, I don't see how you will get out of this house without people seeing, even if you are in disguise. Eurymachos' eyes never leave your door."

Tiberius looked at Longus, who explained for him. "You may not believe what I am about to tell you, but it is a fact [Pliny the Elder, *Natural History,* Book XI.54.143]. The general has miraculous vision – a gift from the gods. He can see at night as others see during the day."

Tiberius added, "It only lasts for a short time after I wake, but it will be long enough for me to get past some prying eyes. We always have the tools we need when destiny requires them."

These last words made Flaccus realize that this mission was more important than they had been led to believe.

In the small hours of the following morning, long before sunrise, Longus helped Tiberius into his disguise – a hooded cloak over an old tunic, with a grimy fleece across his shoulders, a false beard, flecked with gray, weather-beaten leather shoes held together with rags, and a crooked wooden staff.

Tiberius clasped his old friend's elbows in farewell and disappeared into the blackness. He saw his way past Eurymachos' house, and reached the public road before his vision began to dim. There he waited for "dawn's rosy fingers" to guide him into town.

Tiberius selected a merchant ship at the harbor rather than one that favored passengers. He offered a handful of worn silver coins and his labor in exchange for passage to Ephesos.

"What can an old man like you do for me?" was the reply.

Tiberius laid his staff aside and lifted two 75-pound amphorae onto his shoulders as if they were newborn lambs. The ship's captain was impressed. "Welcome aboard, whoever you are."

Meanwhile, at the villa, Tiberius' staff was greeting the day. Longus was in charge, but he was a worried man. The servants and *lictors* were both loyal and unimaginative, but he distrusted Flaccus and Marinus – Flaccus especially. He had always considered them opportunists and nothing more. And the stakes were high - Augustus had forbidden Tiberius to see Vipsania on pain of death.

Marinus did his duty as Tiberius' stand-in – taking his morning exercises and stomping about in character, within the distant view of Eurymachos.

That afternoon, he and Flaccus changed into casual Greek attire and prepared to leave the villa. Longus accosted them.

"Where do you think you're going?"

"Don't you remember? Eurymachos invited us to dine with him," replied Flaccus, with some irritation.

"But Tiberius declined."

"And Tiberius isn't going. We were invited as well. Don't you think it will seem less suspicious if some of us attend?"

Longus thought it over and decided they were right. "Be discreet – no slips."

"Of course not," said Flaccus, but he had plans to be far more than 'indiscreet.' Flaccus knew that Tiberius was up to something, and that he might be able to profit from that knowledge. He and Marinus couldn't investigate while they were under Longus' watchful eye, so he had decided to involve Eurymachos.

After the other guests left the banquet, Flaccus whispered to his host that he and Marinus had a proposition for him. Eurymachos nodded and the three men withdrew into a small room and a jug of wine.

Flaccus got to the point: "Tiberius is gone – he left early this morning, before sunrise."

"What? But I saw him myself at midday."

Marinus sprang to his feet and marched around as Tiberius. Eurymachos understood. "But why? Where?"

"That's what we have to find out," said Flaccus. "He went toward the harbor. How many ships sailed today? Can you find out?"

"No more than a dozen. But surely he was recognized?"

"No, he wore a disguise."

Flaccus leaned forward, staring into Eurymachos' eyes. "That is what interests me. He doesn't want anyone to know he is gone. Why? He claims he just wants to experience life as a common citizen, but there is an urgency about this mission. Tiberius is no rowdy youth, looking to sow some wild oats. Whatever he is doing – he doesn't want Augustus to know about it."

Marinus spoke up. "They say Augustus was furious when he resigned his post. He even complained in the senate that Tiberius was guilty of 'desertion.' Could Tiberius be planning a rebellion? The armies in the north would probably support him after so many seasons under his command."

"That's why we've come to you," continued Flaccus. "We can't leave the villa, but you could follow him. When we know what he's up to, we can decide how to profit from it – all of us."

Eurymachos pushed himself away from the table and stroked his beard. "If you are right, then he would have gone north. No more than 4 or 5 ships would have sailed in that direction today. I'll make some enquiries tomorrow morning."

Flaccus pointed his finger, "Now listen, if you try to cut us out, or betray us, you'll be sorry. If we stick together, we could all do very well from this." The three men clasped hands and nodded in agreement.

Thrasyllus saw that Alcinous was alarmed by this development. "Do you see how trapped he is? Tiberius wanted a simple life, to be anonymous. But everything he has ever done has been watched and weighed, by opportunists as well as the merely curious. Eurymachos was unscrupulous, and he hated Romans, so he pursued the matter with malevolence as well as greed.

"It wasn't long before Eurymachos discovered that a very tall man, dressed like a beggar but with enormous strength, had boarded ship for Ephesos. 'Of course,' he thought, 'he will need funds for an uprising, and Ephesos is the bank of Asia.' Eurymachos realized that if he could prove Tiberius was planning a revolt and present the evidence to the Roman governor, the rewards would be immense.

"In haste, Eurymachos arranged to sail for Ephesos. He had business connections there, with whom he could stay. Perhaps they would have heard whispers of a highborn Roman in the city."

Chapter 19 - Great is Diana of the Ephesians

As Tiberius' ship approached Ephesos, it struck him what a glorious stage the city would be for a reunion. In the center of the harbor was the imposing gate with its many columns and three entrances, two arched and one square. Beyond was the arrow-straight, quarter-mile long colonnade leading to the great theater and the center of the city.

Tiberius wondered which of the three doorways he should choose. Would each one lead to a different destiny?

He entered the central doorway; the square one. Only boldness and directness would do. His heart seemed lodged in his throat as he walked toward the theater. What if he couldn't find her? What if she refused to see him? What if he was discovered and arrested for defying Augustus' orders?

"No," he told his mind. "Boldness and directness! And a disguise."

Ephesos was a bustling, thriving city, with new buildings going up wherever one turned. Everything seemed to be sheathed in marble – even the streets were smooth and white. Tiberius relaxed and realized how easy it would be to blend in with this crowd; everyone was far too busy to notice one more bedraggled stranger. He made arrangements to stay in the sailors' quarter, just inside and west of the main gate. Then he explored the metropolis.

Tiberius soon discovered where Vipsania was living. He knew there would be a small army of attendants and bodyguards to keep shabby-looking men like him away from her. He would have to shadow her movements and watch for an opportunity.

A woman at a tavern told him of the morning visits to the Artemision – he would wait for her there. The temple complex would be crowded with downtrodden pilgrims looking for blessings – he would fit right in.

At the temple in the morning, he climbed the podium steps and took a seat beside the far left front column. From there, he could see the altar and scan the crowds. He watched them pass for hours – but there was no sign of Vipsania. His mind began to drift, lost in thoughts of a possible future.

Vipsania's voice startled him from his daydreams. She was very near. She was behind him, no more than 30 feet away, walking with a group of priestesses around the side of the building.

His chest nearly burst when he saw her; he wanted to embrace her, he almost called her name. But there were too many eyes, too many attendants.

She seemed happy. She was holding hands and sharing a joke with a large woman in a tiara. Tiberius watched them stop a short distance in front of him. A carriage approached and Vipsania climbed in after kissing the priestess goodbye. Tiberius watched helplessly as she drove away.

For a moment, he was paralyzed; his mind a blank. But then the priestess turned toward the temple door and he came to his senses. He hurried down the steps and called after her in Greek, "Holy mother, a moment please. May I ask your indulgence?"

He stopped a short distance from her and bowed obsequiously. She considered him for a moment, then held out her hand: "Come, my child." Her attendants milled about – it was not unusual for a devotee to be granted an audience, to ask for a blessing or to tell a tale of woe.

Tiberius fell to one knee and looked up at her. "The lady who was here – we are acquainted. I... I knew her father." He slipped the Venus ring Vipsania had given him into her hand. "Would you show her this ring and beg her to see me? Privately?"

Artemis understood that the ring was very precious, and she knew this man was a Roman, despite his excellent Greek. She returned the ring to him and said, "Come with me."

Tiberius followed her into the temple, into a corridor that led to a small sitting room. The priestess took a seat there and dismissed her attendants. When they were gone, she looked at him intently. She motioned for him to sit beside her and drew back the hood of his cloak. His professionally trimmed, short hair confirmed her suspicions. "Who are you? What do you want with Vipsania?"

Tiberius said nothing. Artemis understood his reluctance. "Whatever you say in the temple of Artemis is between us and my goddess. Have no fear."

"My name is Tiberius Claudius Nero."

Artemis had suspected, but she was thunderstruck nonetheless. She digested these words for some time. "And what do you want with Vipsania?"

Tiberius knew he could not answer this question directly. "I must see her; I must know that she is safe. I must see her once more and tell her that I am sorry."

Artemis was alarmed. This was not good enough, but she was moved by the pain in Tiberius' eyes – it echoed something she had seen in Vipsania's. She knew that he would not harm her. She decided to help.

"Come to the front of the temple tomorrow, before the end of the 3rd hour. An attendant will lead you into this room. If Vipsania agrees, I will bring her to you."

Tiberius was overcome with gratitude. He took her hand and kissed it. She placed her other hand on his head and said affectionately, "My poor son, you have suffered greatly. May you find peace."

———

Alcinous was impressed. "The priestess was a courageous woman. Defying Augustus, not to mention Gallus. I suppose she was sacrosanct – the high priestess and all. But still, a great risk."

Thrasyllus replied. "I think she knew that Tiberius was genuine. And she knew that Vipsania still loved him."

"So they met at the temple the next morning?"

Thrasyllus had a twinkle in his eye. "Of course not! Life is never that simple."

Alcinous frowned expectantly, but his teacher struggled to his feet, "That's enough for today. Soon it will be supper."

He chuckled to himself as he walked down the path, an exasperated Alcinous grimacing after him.

Today's meal was taken in a very different mood. There was no jesting, no banter. All ears were fixed on a passage from Homer's *Odyssey:* the reunion with Penelope. Her caution, her testing, his impatience to be recognized and accepted - all building to a glorious embrace.

Tiberius wept as he nibbled long slivers of peeled cucumber dipped in oil, sometimes mouthing the words to himself. He knew this part of the story well.

Chapter 20 - A Minor Snag

The following morning, Alcinous hurried along the path, willing Thrasyllus to move more quickly. He was impatient to hear more of Tiberius in Ephesos – he had forgotten all about philosophy.

When they arrived at the statue, Thrasyllus took a moment to gather his thoughts.

"After his meeting with Artemis, Tiberius was energized, but also worried. What if Vipsania wouldn't see him? She might even refuse for his sake, considering the risks.

"It occurred to him that he was filthy and hadn't shaved since he left Rhodes, so he went to the baths, and then the marketplace, where he bought a clean tunic and a more respectable cloak.

"Near the market stalls were the government buildings, with numerous clots of men outside, discussing business and politics. As he passed one of these groups, he heard his own name mentioned. He slowed his pace and listened - what he heard broke his heart.

"'The governor has postponed his visit to Pergamum. He's on his way to Rhodes to pay his respects to Tiberius, who arrived there just a couple of weeks ago.'

"Tiberius took a chance and spoke up, 'Will he be stopping here on his way to Rhodes?' 'No, he is sailing straight from Lesbos. This will disrupt his tax collecting, so he wants to get it done as quickly as possible.' The conversation moved in another direction.

"There was no time to waste; Gallus would be on the fastest ship available. Only an immediate departure with a favorable wind could save Tiberius from discovery."

———

While Tiberius made desperate haste to leave Ephesos, Vipsania joined Artemis for her customary meal at the Artemision. After they dined and most of the other guests had drifted away, the priestess asked familiar questions about her marriage and her feelings for Tiberius. Vipsania wondered why – she had told Artemis all of this before. It upset her.

"Dear Artemis, do you mind if we change the subject? I try not to think about it too much. Tiberius is yesterday."

"And maybe tomorrow," replied the priestess. Vipsania looked blankly at her.

"Vipsania, he is here, in Ephesos! He came to me this morning and showed me a ring – a blue stone with the image of Venus, just as you have described. He wants to see you."

Vipsania reeled. Her head ached and felt heavy, even as her heart swelled.

"It's impossible! How could he be here? Why would he want to see me? It is forbidden!" Her mind raced. "What did you say to him?"

"I told him I would ask you. He will come to the temple tomorrow morning. I said that I would bring you to him if you agree. I made him no promises."

"No! It cannot happen! I couldn't bear it!"

These words escaped somehow, though in her mind she was already in his arms.

"What if someone sees us? What if Gallus finds out?"

"I believe I can promise you secrecy, my dear. There is always a risk. He has taken a great chance in coming here – he is in disguise."

"As what?"

"As a very tall, well-groomed simple shepherd with a noble bearing and a false beard."

Vipsania burst into girlish laughter. She could not stop. The mental image of Tiberius in a ridiculous disguise released all the excitement, fear, and elation that had built up within her. She began to weep. She looked into Artemis' eyes and sobbed through her words, "Should I see him? Can I see him?"

"I think you must, Vipsania. But sleep on it first. Perhaps the goddess will guide you. If you decide against it, I believe he will understand."

Vipsania did not sleep at all that night. She decided she would see him, and then she could not wait, pleading with the sun to rise early. Wondering where Tiberius was at every moment – thrilled to think that she was breathing the same smoky air.

In the morning, she wore her Trojan horse pendant. She wanted to look her best, but couldn't sit still for the *ornatrix* to do her hair properly. She knew it didn't matter – Tiberius would be wearing rags and a beard!

The ride to the temple took longer than she could imagine; the chariot wheels seemed to spin backwards. She hurried into the temple – her attendants couldn't keep up with her. Her eyes darted from face to face. He could have been anyone, anywhere. Where was he?

Finally, Vipsania saw Artemis moving towards her. The priestess took Vipsania to one side, finally whispering, "He has not come. I do not know why. Something must have happened."

Vipsania exhaled – but she couldn't find a way to breathe in again. She simply couldn't breathe. Her mind went blank. Artemis guided her to a marble bench and sat with her for a moment.

Suddenly, she was composed. She looked at her friend and felt a little embarrassed. She thought she had accepted what had happened to her life and moved on. Now she knew better.

Artemis held her hand. "I'm so sorry. I'm certain he will explain when he can. There was a reason for this."

Vipsania replied softly. "Yes, there was a reason. I had forgotten how much I love him."

———

Alcinous interrupted - he had to know immediately: "Did his ship arrive in Rhodes before Gallus?"

"No," replied Thrasyllus, "The governor's ship was in the harbor when Tiberius arrived. But Longus intercepted Gallus and distracted him with a tour of the city and harbor facilities. Gallus protested that he was tired after the voyage and anxious to see Tiberius and then rest. 'Where is he staying? Perhaps he can accommodate my party?'

"Longus was cornered. 'Tiberius is staying at a small villa nearby, but he has gone hunting in the hills. His villa is on the property of a local magistrate, a man named Eurymachos, who is out of town at the moment. Why don't you move into Eurymachos' house? I will let you know as soon as Tiberius has returned.'

"Gallus was irritated but too worn out to argue."

———

Not knowing that Eurymachos was away, Tiberius waited for nightfall before attempting a return to his villa. He found a very relieved and shaken

Longus pacing in front of the entrance.

"Thank the gods, you have returned!"

"Am I in time?" Tiberius asked breathlessly.

"Only just – he is in Eurymachos' house tonight. He plans to look for you tomorrow. I told him you were hunting."

"Where is Eurymachos? Did he suspect?"

"He went away on business just after you left – we've heard nothing of him."

The next morning, Gallus stormed the villa with his retainers, determined to see Tiberius. He was ushered into the reception room. Tiberius was seated, wearing a toga, his *lictors* and other attendants standing on either side of him.

Gallus was well aware that Tiberius outranked him – hence his journey to Rhodes. It was the necessary gesture. Also, he was curious to know what political role Tiberius would play in the East.

The greetings were stiff and insincere – these men despised each other.

Gallus was direct: "Will you be requiring my assistance during your mission here?"

Tiberius replied flatly, "I have no mission. I am retired. I do not intend to visit your province, nor any other. I have come here to study and to rest, that is all."

Gallus didn't believe him. He thought of Vipsania. He lied. "Vipsania knows you are here. She sends you no greeting – she is very busy with our children, engrossed in her new life. We are very happy."

Tiberius stood up abruptly and walked Gallus to the door. "It grieves me that you interrupted your duties to come here. I assure you, I will not interfere in your administration. Have a safe voyage to ... where do you go from here?"

"To Pergamum, to continue my tour of the province."

"May you arrive there safely, and serve Rome well."

The two men saluted formally and Gallus left – a week at sea for a 10 minute meeting!

A few moments later, the room had cleared, leaving only Tiberius and Longus.

"What will you do now?" asked Longus.

"Kill myself!" Tiberius glanced in exasperation at his friend. "I think I would if I had to live with that man. Poor Vipsania!"

"Did you see her?"

"Yes, I saw her, but she didn't see me. I was hoping to meet with her when I heard about Gallus. She knows by now that I was in Ephesos. I have to go back, Longus - as soon as Gallus is safely away."

Chapter 21 - Second Try

News finally reached Vipsania of Tiberius' retirement to Rhodes – and of Gallus' journey to meet with him there. She understood why Tiberius left Ephesos so suddenly. She lingered longer at the temple each day, knowing that he had been there, hoping that he would return.

Meanwhile, Eurymachos had spent many days scouring the city, looking for him. He was furious when he heard that Gallus had gone to meet Tiberius in Rhodes - that he had missed an opportunity to cultivate the governor of Asia! He cursed Flaccus and Marinus for sending him on this wild goose chase.

In an effort to salvage (and explain) his trip, he spent a few days renewing business acquaintances. Still, he felt foolish as he neared the harbor gate, preparing to board ship for Rhodes.

He recognized a galley from home by its sails, and took the right archway, farthest away, to avoid meeting anyone he might know. As he passed through, his eyes were caught by a tall bearded man, coming directly towards him. He was stooped and shabbily dressed, but with a familiar-looking nose and brow. A shiver passed through Eurymachos: "By Zeus, it's Tiberius!" His plans suddenly changed.

As her carriage rolled toward the temple, Vipsania struggled to regain the happiness she had felt before Tiberius' visit. But the lost prospect of seeing him had left her with a melancholy that even the temple couldn't relieve.

When Artemis joined her after the ceremony, Vipsania was not in the mood for pleasantries. She began to make her apologies and return to the city, but her friend had made plans. Trailing a group of attendants, the priestess led them into a grove of trees. A picnic perhaps?

There was a circle of marble benches beneath a giant cedar. Vipsania dutifully took a seat and Artemis moved away, "Wait here for a moment." She signaled to the attendants to follow her. Vipsania gazed up into the great tree; not in the mood for surprises.

Gradually, she sensed a man nearby, looking at her. She didn't turn towards him. She gripped the bench with both hands and a tremble rippled through her. Could it be?

Tiberius lowered his hood and stripped off his beard as he moved into view. They gazed at each other, their eyes glistening.

He sat beside her, softly molding her cheeks with his fingers, as if to confirm that she was real. They embraced; they looked at each other in amazement. Neither spoke – it would have measured the moment. It had been three years since Tiberius had followed her litter through the streets of Rome.

For a very long time, they sat together, stroking each other, healing each other's wounds. Much was said in silence. At last, Artemis appeared, moving tentatively towards them. Tiberius looked up and said "Thank you!"

She shook her head, "It is nothing. But you will want time alone. I have an apartment, not far from here. No one goes there – it is my escape. Let me show you."

It was very modest – just a room and a half above the stables. But it was clean, and private. It was sparsely furnished – there was a bed. For the next three afternoons, it was their home. They never spoke of the future, until the third day when Tiberius brought it up.

"We must be together, Vipsania. There is a way. Come with me to Parthia! I have connections there. We can sail to Antioch and cross the frontier with a caravan. The Parthians are civilized people; they will treat us well."

For a moment, Vipsania was tempted. But she knew it would be a mistake. "We would never see Drusus again. I would never see my children again. They would be at the mercy of Julia and Gallus. And you would become nothing but a curiosity and a pawn in the Parthian court, like Demaratus with Xerxes. You would be miserable!"

"I am miserable without you, Vipsania. We would be together."

"You are destined for greatness, my love. You would be trading a life of achievement for one of inactivity and powerlessness."

Tiberius was in earnest, "Don't you see? I have already given up all of that to be with you. I left Julia. I defied Augustus. It was the only way I could atone for what I did to you, what I did to us."

Vipsania struggled to remain sensible. "No! You cannot change what has happened, my love. We cannot go back. Drusus' future, my children's futures - everything depends on what we do now!"

"Are you happy with Gallus? Is that it?"

Vipsania nearly choked. "No, NO! You know I am not! I am just one of his possessions. He thinks to himself: this statue once belonged to Crassus, this table to Mark Antony, this woman to Tiberius. But he is not cruel; he does not beat me."

Tiberius gave her an ironic look. Vipsania ignored it and went on. "My love, there is more to life than happiness. We have children, and duties – to ourselves as well as to them. We would live to regret it. And then we would resent each other; our feelings for each other would change."

Tiberius was devastated, but he could not argue with her.

"There is hope," she continued. "Life is uncertain. No one knows what the future holds, except maybe your stars. Did they tell you we should live in Parthia?"

Tiberius looked down. "No. They predict only military victory, political success, and domestic misery. I was trying to alter fate, to seize control of our lives. I guess I knew it was hopeless."

Vipsania kissed him tenderly. "Not hopeless, my love. And we have these fresh memories to see us through. Remember, we are always together in our hearts.”

Tiberius nodded gravely. She lifted his chin and kissed him gently, he attempted to smile.

———

Thrasyllus wrestled to his feet and walked to and fro, trying to loosen his joints.

“That night, they stayed in the apartment together. In the early morning, Tiberius took his leave, adjusting his beard as he walked away. But a man was watching from one of the stable stalls. It was Eurymachos! He had been following Tiberius since he spotted him at the harbor. He saw him with Vipsania in the grove; he saw them enter the apartment each day.

“Eurymachos knew that Tiberius would kill him if he approached. After all, this was a man who had given up an empire; he could not be blackmailed. Vipsania, however, might be an easier mark.

“As soon as Tiberius was out of sight, Eurymachos approached the apartment. He knocked on the door. Vipsania thought it was Tiberius, back for one last kiss, so she opened it. She was startled to see a stranger: ’My lady, you have had a very important visitor, I believe.’

“She felt nauseous. ‘What do you want?’ ‘Your patronage, my lady.’ ‘That is a matter for my husband and he is away.’ ‘I do not think you want your husband involved in this. The emperor would pay a great deal for this information. Everyone knows Tiberius is forbidden to see you.’

“Vipsania looked around to be sure there was no one else watching. ‘Come inside,’ she said.”

Chapter 22 - Despair (5 BC)

Tiberius dragged his heart back to Rhodes. All of his energy had been invested in the reunion and escape with Vipsania, and now that was over. There was no future that interested him. He was an exile without hope of reprieve. He didn’t even want to return to Rome, to his former life. He was only 36 years old, but he felt much older. He turned to philosophy.

Thrasyllus explained “He began to attend lectures and symposia in Rhodes. He insisted that he be treated as a regular student; that he would never learn unless people were free to correct and criticize him. He promised impartiality, and that anyone could disagree with him with impunity.

"As time went on and he continued to behave as a humble student, to dress as a Greek and go places without his attendants, never using his powers as a Roman magistrate, people began to take him at his word. In fact, he was sometimes treated roughly.

"There was a professor of literature there, a man named Diogenes. Tiberius was anxious to attend his lectures, but this man only taught on the seventh day of the week. Tiberius came to his house on another day and requested a special session. Diogenes didn't even greet him – he sent a slave to tell Tiberius to come back on the seventh day."

"How did he react?" asked Alcinous.

"Tiberius? He came back on the seventh day! But many years later, when Tiberius was emperor, Diogenes came to Rome. He decided to visit his former student. When he arrived at the palace and asked to see Tiberius, the answer was to the point:

"'Come back in the seventh year.'"

Alcinous laughed out loud.

"Remember this," Thrasyllus said in a serious tone, "Tiberius never forgets anything."

"He only asserted himself once in Rhodes. It was at a symposium. Two sophists became locked in an argument about destiny. One was an Epicurean - he insisted that the course of human life was entirely dependent on the exercise of free will. His opponent was a stoic who held that worldly circumstances were determined by the gods. He argued that a man could not change his destiny, so he should embrace it and never let misfortune spoil his equanimity.

"The epicurean scoffed at the stoic: 'You superstitious Stoics are all the same, thinking that the gods determine fate. Nonsense! Look around you man! Chaos! If the gods are this disorganized, why should we call them gods?'

"To which the stoic replied: 'Everything is determined by the gods, even if you do not have the subtlety to see it. No man can change his destiny, so he should embrace it and remain calm at all times. He should strive, of course, as if his free will could triumph. But nothing will come to pass unless the gods approve.'

"This was what Tiberius wanted to hear. It was an idea he could rebuild his life upon. But the opinion of the audience – mostly brash young noblemen - was going in the other direction.

"Finally, Tiberius spoke up: 'For me, Homer presents the world as it truly is. What choices did Odysseus have? Agamemnon forced him to leave his wife and son and go to war. He longed to return to Penelope, but he was thwarted by fate, condemned to wander for 10 years before he could go home. This is the way it is with mortals – our lives are determined by forces beyond our control!'

"A heavy-set young man scoffed at him. 'So a Roman would lecture us Greeks on Homer! And what a strange example! Odysseus, the very model of free will! You say he longed to return to Penelope – then why did he dally with so many other women?'

"Tiberius countered, 'Calypso held him prisoner against his will.' "'Yes, but they had children together – he can't have been too miserable with her. And he chose to stay for a year with Circe - and he chose to go to Troy in the first place. Our choices may be difficult, but we make them; we set the priorities. Why, even Penelope – she could have left the palace and searched for her husband. She stayed with the suitors because it was easy, because she was attached to comfort and wealth.'"

Thrasyllus continued, "The man didn't notice how Tiberius' was reacting to his words. He went on, 'And what about the Cyclops? Perhaps destiny led Odysseus to the cave, but it was his reason, his free will that got him out of it. He chose to succeed, and so he succeeded. Failure is a choice, too.'

"Tiberius was certain that the man was really talking about Julia, Vipsania, and Tiberius himself. He responded slowly and gravely, knowing that his words would be ridiculed:

"'Whatever room for free will Odysseus had... (a long pause)... was determined by his destiny.'

"It was the punch line. The room exploded with laughter. Several members of the audience congratulated the man who had humiliated the famous Roman.

"Tiberius stormed out of the room, mounted his horse, and rode to the villa. By the time he arrived, he was purple with rage, convinced that the attack had been personal. He marched inside like a general in a crisis: 'Everyone to his post! I am convening a tribunal in the city. At once!'

"The *lictors* scrambled to find their *fasces*. Marinus and Flaccus worried that Tiberius had heard of their plot with Eurymachos. They fumbled as they donned their togas, scrambling to catch up with Tiberius.

"His entourage marched to the hall where the symposium was being held. Tiberius pointed at his tormentor: 'Seize that man!' The *lictors* dragged him out the door to a hastily devised courtroom on the building steps.

"Tiberius was prosecutor, judge, and jury: 'This tribunal is in session. This man is charged with disrespect for the majesty of the senate and the people of Rome in the person of a duly appointed tribune of the people. He is hereby sentenced to imprisonment, the duration to be determined at a later date.'

"Then, with delicious sarcasm, he said, 'Let it be recorded that the people's tribune passes this sentence in accordance with his official duties, which have been given to him by a higher power, and not as an expression of his free will. Take him away.'

"The man was indeed thrown into prison, but Tiberius regretted his impulse almost at once and ordered his release the following morning. This was a low point for Tiberius – an act inspired by grief, despair, and wounded pride. Even today, he winces at the memory. It took months for him to regain his ease among the Rhodians, and they never trusted him again."

Chapter 23 - Pregnant in Asia

Vipsania felt numb after seeing Tiberius. The illusion of freedom from her husband was gone – and now she was the slave of another, much more sinister man.

The blackmail required her to sell all her properties in the East, which she had inherited from her father. But it was a price she would gladly pay if scandal could be avoided. Gallus would not be pleased to hear of her infidelity – but if Augustus learned that Tiberius deserted Rome to cheat on his daughter with a woman he was forbidden to see - who could predict his reaction? Tiberius might even be executed.

Dreadful thoughts swirled through her mind. She was always tired; worn out from thinking. Only sleep brought relief from her torment. But sleep made the days and weeks before Gallus' return pass more quickly.

And then she realized she was pregnant.

With her family and friends in Rome, Vipsania had only Artemis to confide in. She did not burden her with the tale of Eurymachos – the priestess would feel responsible, and Vipsania didn't want that. But she had to share her feelings about the baby with someone.

Vipsania answered the unasked question: "Yes, I have thought about abortion – then Gallus would never know."

Artemis was cautious. "I understand there are excellent physicians in Ephesos who perform the operation. There would be very little risk"

Vipsania leaned forward and spoke with feeling: "I cannot do it, Artemis, even though it would be so much easier for me. This is Tiberius' child - our child. It seems a miracle for us to be connected in this way again. I cannot put an end to that, whatever the consequences. There is joy as well as dread in my heart because of this – my only real fear is for the child's future."

"Could Gallus think it is his?"

"No, we haven't been together in months. He didn't want me to be pregnant in Asia. He said it was so I could stand the travel better, but he wanted to show me off. A large belly would have been a blemish. He will be furious, of course – he will expose the child."

She suddenly grasped Artemis' thigh and implored her, "Promise me you will arrange for its care?"

Her friend held her hand reassuringly. "Of course, my dear. We will bring it to the temple and look after it until I can find a good home. You have my solemn vow."

Vipsania was relieved. "But the child must never know who its parents are. It would be a curse. My hope is that it will have a simple, happy life. The life that Tiberius and I always wanted, without the shackles of high birth."

When Gallus returned to Ephesos after harvesting his taxes, he was in a cheerful mood. His tour of the province had been very lucrative and Tiberius was out of the way on Rhodes. He took little notice of Vipsania, much to her relief. But Syriacus, a close friend of his who had just arrived from Rome, was more observant.

"I see you are expecting another child, Gallus. Congratulations! May it be a son!"

"What are you talking about, Vipsania is not pregnant!"

"I believe you will find that she is."

Gallus confronted Vipsania. When she confessed to the pregnancy, he struck her across the face, his signet ring drawing blood. She fell to her hands and knees.

In a way, Gallus was pleased. The high-minded wife of the great Tiberius was nothing but a whore! He no longer cared that he had never won her heart away from his rival. Now she had given it to ... whom? A soldier or a tradesman, he chose to believe. Maybe even a slave?

She refused to tell him who it was. Syriacus suggested torture, but even a lashing administered by Gallus' officers failed to open her lips. Inadvertently, Gallus selected the most effective punishment of all.

"Whoever he is, you will never see him again. I'm taking you to Sardis with me. Your confinement will be total and you will have the child there in secret. I'll not have my reputation soiled by your degradation!"

Vipsania was stunned. Artemis would not be able to save her child after all!

When the baby girl was born, Gallus insisted on the usual formalities. He came to Vipsania's chamber to see the infant, which was laid at his feet. It was customary for a Roman father to acknowledge his offspring by lifting it up in his arms. Instead, Gallus barely glanced at the girl and said laconically, "No, I will not raise this one." Then, turning to his attendant, "Have the child exposed."

Vipsania, reeling from childbirth, knew what Gallus would say, but still the words hit hard. She had but a few moments with her baby – time to say a prayer, to wrap her in a green blanket and loop the Trojan horse pendant that Tiberius had given her around the child's neck. These were all the protection she could give her. And then a servant whisked her baby away.

Vipsania was dazed, disoriented, blinded by tears. When she regained her wits, she rushed to the window, hoping to catch a final glimpse - perhaps even see someone claim her baby. Then she realized she could hear her, crying in the distance. She broke out in goose flesh, her nipples ached.

The house was on a hillside, overlooking a crossroads in the center of town. She strained to see through the louvered blind. At last she spotted a smudge of green at the foot of a column, a couple of hundred feet away.

For hours, Vipsania listened as the cries become fainter, then intermittent. She ran out of tears and began to tear at her forearms with a hairpin; anything to relieve the unrelenting pain - even more pain.

By dusk, the cries were hollow, barely audible. There were long silences. Then it was dark. She watched for passersby carrying torches or lamps, hoping to see... but the shadow of the column was all she could make out.

Exhausted, she dozed, her brow against the window frame; then she awakened to more crying. It grew louder. Then it stopped!

Desperate, she pushed against the blind, trying to widen the gap. Suddenly, miraculously, she could see them clearly, as if they were close at hand: two figures with torches, standing near the column. They lingered, and then they moved away. There were no more cries or whimpers.

Vipsania took it in – her baby had been saved! She let out a cry that surprised and thrilled her; it came from a place deep within. She found fresh tears – of joy. Her prayers had been answered. Never had she felt more love for the gods. In her mind, she spoke to Tiberius: "She lives! Our baby lives!"

———

Alcinous wasn't ashamed of his tears. Thrasyllus fell silent and shed a few of his own. "Enough for today, my friend. Enough."

Chapter 24 - A Lighter Mood (AD 36)

Today's banquet was a celebration of Augustus' birthday – the 23rd of September - organized by the first emperor's grandson Caligula. A life-sized silver statue of Augustus, crowned with a golden laurel wreath, stood at the place of honor.

All of the guests had been given costumes of gods and heroes. Tiberius, of course, was dressed as Jupiter. Alcinous became Theseus while Thrasyllus donned the robes of the seer Teiresias. His wife Aka, a former princess of Commagene, had become Andromache, the wife of Hector. Caligula himself was dressed as Mercury.

Tiberius was in good spirits and congratulated Caligula on the arrangements. "Augustus enjoyed costume parties like this, though he was criticized for it. It's amazing how one is influenced by wearing a costume. Why, suddenly I feel like hurling thunderbolts!" He raised his left fist above his head, looking for a target. Everyone laughed – and laughed again when a musician struck his cymbal.

A stream of actors and dancers entered the room and performed a pantomime while the guests ate and drank in honor of the deified Augustus. One of the actors, wearing emperor's robes and a false nose as big as a shark's fin, was clearly meant to be Tiberius. He was dragging around what looked like an enormous cucumber, as long as he was tall.

At the opposite end of the room appeared an impressively large, helmeted woman, holding a long scepter. She was Roma personified – but actually Macro, the prefect of the Praetorian Guard, in woman's clothing.

Roma looked longingly at "Tiberius" and held out her arms to him. "Tiberius" returned the gesture, folded his hands over his heart, and signaled to his heralds. They blew their horns and "the emperor" crouched like a sprinter at the starting block, adjusting his position over and over. He stood up and ran in place, wiping the sweat from his brow, never actually moving forward.

Alcinous laughed with everyone else, but needed Thrasyllus to explain: "He's lampooning the emperor for saying he will visit Rome, but never actually going there. The man is the emperor's *derisor* – making fun of Tiberius is his job. It's quite all right if he does it good-naturedly. It's a traditional Roman way to humble the great so the gods won't resent them."

"I heard that Tiberius banished all actors from Italy."

"That is true – but there was nothing good-natured about their behavior. Most of these men are his own servants."

Caligula couldn't seem to decide whether he was a dancer or a diner, so he settled for both, twirling around the room with goblet in hand. He pulled his corpulent friend Aulus Vitellius (who, like Caligula, would be an emperor someday) to join him in the performance. Vitellius as a portly Vulcan and the tall, thin, ungainly Caligula made quite a pair.

Alcinous was charmed by the young prince, amazed by his energy and good spirits. Thrasyllus noticed this and leaned towards him: "The prince is full of fun, but don't be deceived. He is ambitious, and not to be crossed. He dislikes me for what I said about his chances of succeeding to the throne: 'Caligula has as much chance of being emperor as of riding his horse across the Bay of Baiae.' And now he is almost certain to rule. It might be convenient if I die before Tiberius does. Fortunately, the stars assure me that I will."

This aside reminded Alcinous of the dangerous political undercurrents on Capri.

The excitement and gaiety soon ran their course and Tiberius began a scholarly discussion of obscure Roman religious practices. For Alcinous, watching "the gods" discuss religion had its own amusements.

Chapter 25 - Home Again (5 BC)

The following afternoon, Thrasyllus picked up the threads of his tale. "Let us see. Gallus' year as proconsul of Asia came to an end a few weeks after the baby girl was born. Vipsania knew that he would tell his parents of her 'indiscretion' when they returned home, and that Salonina would discover new ways to punish and humiliate her. But the memory of her time with Tiberius, and the knowledge that their daughter was alive in Asia, made all of this more than bearable. And she cherished the uneasy hope that Eurymachos' tentacles wouldn't reach all the way to Rome."

———

Vipsania longed to see Drusus, now nine years old, but it was weeks before she was allowed to go. When she finally saw him, she was heartbroken by the changes in her son. Julia and her circle had made him arrogant and spoiled and taught him disdain for his real parents. He was aloof and impatient with Vipsania, seemingly put out that he had to spend time with her at all. His words were chosen to wound her: "I hear Father is sulking in Rhodes, all washed up. And Augustus will never let him come back.'"

"Your father is a great man and Augustus needs him. He is taking a well-deserved break; that is all. He will come back some day. I know he longs to see you."

"That's a lie; he could have taken me with him!" Drusus was ashamed that tears came to his eyes – he wiped them away quickly.

"No," insisted his mother, "he knows that you are happier here in Rome."

She knew that Tiberius loved his son, but also that he had been prepared to leave him and never see him again. For the first time, she admitted to herself what a foolish, selfish act the retirement was, and that Drusus was its principal victim. She felt Tiberius' shame. She could not defend him with conviction. Drusus sensed this.

"It doesn't matter anyway,' he said. "I am happier here in Rome. I don't care if I never see him again."

Vipsania changed the subject. "How are your studies? How do you like to spend your time?"

"Study is boring. I like the games! I know a few of the best gladiators! I saw one of them get killed a few days ago – the blood spurted from his neck like a fountain!"

Vipsania was aghast: "You attend the games? They let you attend the games?"

"Of course! Augustus says it will make me ready to be a soldier; it will teach me how to kill and how to die. He says he needs soldiers. Even more since Father deserted him."

As Vipsania left Julia's residence; teeming with dignitaries, actors, gladiators, and all sorts of people; she was approached by a man she knew, a senator named Sextus Vestilius.

"Pardon me, lady Vipsania, but there is a business matter I wish to discuss with you. Forgive me for bringing this up in such a place, but I am told you will prefer it this way."

Vipsania was perplexed. She followed him to a quiet corner.

"There is a Greek who owes me a great deal of money. A man named Eurymachos of Rhodes."

Vipsania's heart seemed to stop.

"He says that you are acquainted with him and that you will gladly satisfy his obligations, but that I shouldn't let your husband know of our arrangement. Have I done wrong in approaching you?"

Sextus appeared to be entirely innocent of the true circumstances. He was an old friend of Tiberius' brother Drusus, and, through him, had become a close associate of Tiberius. Vipsania could not let him suspect that anything was amiss.

"What is the sum that he owes you?" "A million sesterces."

Vipsania was staggered. "I cannot cover that amount."

"I understand, but Eurymachos said you would be willing to pay the interest, while he arranges for the payment of principal."

"How much would you need?"

"Only 100,000 a year."

It was more than her total income from her remaining properties.

"When will you need the money?"

"We agreed that interest would be paid every other month. I can have my accountant make the arrangements with your accountant. There is no hurry – we can begin next month. And I will let you know as soon as Eurymachos has repaid me, of course."

Vipsania knew that day would never come. But there was no choice – Tiberius' life might be at stake!

Chapter 26 - The Exile

When Tiberius heard that Gallus and Vipsania had returned to Rome, he felt like a castaway. Part of him wanted to follow, but his pride and Augustus' anger made this impossible. Besides, he had no desire to resume his life as a general and "assistant emperor" – nor as Julia's husband. He decided to make the best of his situation.

His days were regimented – regular exercise and target practice with spear and javelin at the parade ground, horseback riding, extensive reading and attendance at lectures and symposia. He resumed his studies with the rhetorician Theodore of Gadara, one of his former teachers in Rome.

Theodore was a master of political oratory, which it appeared Tiberius would have little use for now. Nevertheless, he was fascinated by the teacher's approach:

"While making speeches in the courtroom or the assembly, or even when doing business in the marketplace, to be brief and to the point is not always necessary or appropriate or even advisable. Your opponents will find ready targets in your words and they will pounce. They will twist your statements to suit their purposes and then hold you to them. If, on the other hand, you obscure your meaning and prolong your delivery as much as possible, choosing ten words when three would suffice, or twenty words when ten would suffice, or one hundred words when twenty would suffice, then they will become confused and forgetful – and therefore much more prone to compromise."

It was a lesson that Tiberius would learn well and often apply, to the great frustration of his contemporaries.

He also took a keen interest in the local artistic traditions. The dramatic sculptures, typified by the famous *Laocoon,* often depicted mythological scenes of great anguish and emotional intensity. Tiberius was fascinated by them; they seemed to express his own inner turmoil. Years later, he would adorn his villas with masterpieces from the hands of Rhodian artists.

He tried his hand at many things – even painting and sculpture, but soon discovered he had more thumbs than fingers. So he wrote poetry, in both Greek and Latin. Tiberius also sponsored four-horse chariots at the games in Olympia and Thespiae – his team even became Olympic champion!

His social calendar was crowded - Tiberius was a local attraction, like the ruins of the Colossus. Every dignitary who sailed near Rhodes had to visit the famous general.

And so the months and years trickled by. Tiberius began to feel truly retired. News of events in Rome reached his ears, but they no longer interested him. Gaius and Lucius were named "princes of the youth," marking them as Augustus' heirs. It rankled somewhat that he was being replaced by a pair of boys, but he knew they would be preferred eventually – better that it should happen in his absence.

Let Gaius and Lucius deal with the Germans, he thought, and with the Roman mob. He was well out of it! He missed his son, and Vipsania, of course, but the aversions exceeded the attractions. He could spend the rest of his life on Rhodes.

These thoughts did not prepare him for the thunderbolt when it came – or his reactions to it.

Chapter 27 - The Fall of Julia (2 BC)

Rumors flew like sea gulls through the city of Rhodes: Augustus had banished Julia! He had learned of her sexual misdeeds and exiled her to the tiny island of Pandateria!

Tiberius was galvanized – impatient to hear what had really happened. Finally a letter arrived from Livia:

"My dear son. Rome is in uproar; Julia is disgraced! She has been sent away by Augustus. Many of her lovers and cronies have been punished. Sempronius Gracchus has been exiled. Iullus Antonius, Mark Antony's son, has committed suicide.

"You will hear that she has been accused of 'numerous adulteries and immoral behavior,' which have only now been discovered by Augustus. The truth is much more sinister. She was at the center of a plot to over-throw the government!

"The ramifications will become clearer as time goes on, but you will be anxious to know where you stand, and what has become of Drusus. He has been taken into the family of Gaius Asinius Gallus, much to Vipsania's relief. Gallus says that he will treat him as his own son.

"Julia's misdeeds have put you in a better light with Augustus. He has signed a bill of divorce in your name, freeing you from further obligation to her. But he will not let you return to Rome, Tiberius, should you wish to. Your tribunician power would overshadow Gaius and Lucius and he wants their preeminence to be clear. Also, he has not forgiven you for leav-ing against his orders, though I think he now has a better understanding of what it was to be Julia's husband."

Tiberius' hands trembled as he read the letter. His former life and aspi-rations were not as far behind him as he had supposed. He paced furiously through the villa's courtyard, but his agitation only increased. He had to get away and think.

He mounted his horse and rode into the high country. He rode until his horse choked for air. Then he dismounted, sat on a boulder with a majestic view of the island and the sea beyond, and contemplated the future. Rome without Julia! Divorced! Even if Augustus recalled her, the marriage was over. For the first time in 4 years, Tiberius thought seriously about going home.

———

Alcinous was surprised by these revelations. "Julia plotted to overthrow Augustus? I heard only about her sex life."

Thrasyllus replied, "Julia had always been promiscuous. After the separation from Tiberius, there were more lovers than ever. Augustus knew about them; he was well aware that his daughter had inherited his hearty sexual appetite. But he pretended not to notice. Political intrigue was something else altogether. He never forgave her for contemplating his removal – especially with a son of his old rival Mark Antony!"

"Tiberius wrote the obligatory letters to Augustus, asking him to forgive Julia, insisting that she be allowed to keep the gifts Tiberius had given her, begging him to allow her to return to Rome. This was the proper thing for a husband to do, so he did it. The letters were received with no more seriousness than they were written."

———

For Vipsania, Julia's destruction was a wonderful boon, in more ways than one. She moved quickly to rescue Drusus from the chaos at Julia's house. Her son would now live with her! She only hoped that, at age 12, he wasn't too old to be influenced. She hoped he would grow close to her children with Gallus – two sons and two daughters, with four more sons yet to come.

Of course, Gallus was more than happy to add the grandson of Livia to his household. "Now you have all your children together," observed Salonina, as if this was a favor she didn't deserve. "All but one," thought Vipsania to herself.

She was also relieved that Tiberius had been freed from a broken, unhappy marriage. Vipsania passed over her jealous impulses and prayed sincerely, genuinely, that he would find happiness with another woman.

The final benefit came with an element of risk. Vipsania reasoned that, with Julia disgraced, Augustus wouldn't care that Tiberius had betrayed her by visiting his first wife a thousand miles from Rome. So she gathered her courage and told her accountant to inform Sextus Vestilius that she would no longer be making payments. Then she waited with bated breath for a reaction. It never came. After three years of pinching coppers and fearing worse, it was over!

Chapter 28 - Waiting

For Tiberius, time seemed almost to stop. The more seriously he contemplated a return to the capital, the more slowly the weeks and months seemed to go by. Finally, the greatest obstacle was removed – his powers as a tribune expired. He could no longer be seen as a threat to Gaius and Lucius because of his rank.

He composed a letter to the emperor - his first serious attempt at communication with Augustus since coming to Rhodes, and much more difficult than he expected. Tiberius realized that he could not tell the truth. To admit that he left Rome to run away to Parthia with Vipsania would not do.

His writing desk was soon littered with discarded scrolls. Finally, he settled for not quite right:

"... I know that you were displeased by my retirement, that you felt I had abandoned my responsibilities. However, now that your sons Gaius and Lucius (Augustus had adopted his grandsons) are grown men, I am able to confess the true reasons for my departure.

"It was clear to me that you intended for Gaius and Lucius to be without rivals, so that they would be your clear successors as the first men in Rome. I knew that I might be seen as standing in their way, so I thought it best to remove myself and allow them to come into their own as your undoubted heirs. Now that this has happened, I beg you to allow me to return to my home and see the members of my family, whom I greatly miss..."

The days passed even more slowly while he waited for Augustus' response. When it came, he was afraid to read it. He rode into the high country, to his boulder, and pulled the scroll open, only letting himself see one line at a time:

"Your letter requesting permission to return to Rome has been received by me...

"Concerning the members of your family, whom you were so eager to leave...

"Abandon all hope of seeing them, or the city of your birth, ever again...

"You have made your bed; now lie in it!"

At first Tiberius felt shame – to be dismissed so coldly by a man he admired, even loved. But rage soon overwhelmed him. He stood up and threw the scroll as far as he could, then he fired a dozen rocks in its direction.

A wave of fear ran through him: he was as much an exile as Julia now, without a post or official office. He was vulnerable.

———

Thrasyllus raised a finger for emphasis. "But Tiberius was the son of Livia. And she would not let him be in danger. Within days, another letter arrived from Rome, granting him the status of 'ambassador.' This involved no duties and very little prestige, but it conferred some dignity. Livia had argued this concession out of Augustus. Tiberius was relieved, but he soon discovered how little protection it gave him.

"As word spread that Tiberius, bereft of his powers, had been rejected by Augustus, his enemies became bolder. At first he noticed subtle differences. Services that had been given freely by local tradesmen in Rhodes now came at a price. Eurymachos began charging rent for his villa, claiming that he had suffered a 'financial reverse.' Tiberius noticed that people muttered and laughed among themselves when he passed. The look of awe and respect was gone, replaced by amusement and even contempt.

"His circle of followers grew smaller. The *lictors* and other attendants evaporated when his tribunician power expired. Several of the knights who lived with him in Rhodes, including Marinus and Flaccus, eventually found themselves 'called away on business.' Only Longus remained unequivocally loyal.

Thrasyllus continued, "It was at this time that Tiberius became even more obsessed with the stars. He constructed a small observatory on a cliff by the sea and tried to discern his future with the help of astrologers. As you know, this was when I first came to know him. He was a restless, anxious man, convinced that he was in great danger.

"His fears increased tenfold when Gaius, 19 years old, came to Asia with absolute power over the eastern provinces. His mission was to deal with the Parthians and Armenians, as Tiberius had done at about the same age. For the first time, Tiberius was clearly subordinate to one of Julia's sons – and he knew that Gaius' entourage included men who despised him. One of them in particular, Marcus Lollius, nursed an old grudge.

"Sixteen years earlier, Lollius had been the governor of Gaul. He suffered a minor defeat at the hands of the Germans in which one of the legionary standards was captured - a shameful disgrace for any Roman commander. Augustus and Tiberius had gone to Gaul to assess the situation. Lollius was dismissed from his post and replaced by Tiberius – an insult that Lollius never forgot. And now he was in a position to take revenge.

"Lollius told Gaius that he should not rely on soldiers who had previously served under Tiberius. He told him that several of Tiberius' former centurions had returned from leave with seditious intentions. 'These men must have consulted their old commander and been told to foment rebellion on his behalf!' Gaius didn't quite believe it, but he reported the accusations to the emperor.

"To his horror, Tiberius received a letter from Augustus, warning him not to interfere with the army or Gaius in any way: 'Make no mistake, Gaius is my representative, with the power of life and death over all of my eastern subjects. Anyone who seeks to undermine his authority will pay with his life.'

"Tiberius fired back, 'If you doubt my loyalty, send a responsible man, someone you can trust, to observe my behavior. Assign someone to monitor my words and actions, so that you can be certain of my reliability.'

"There was no response."

Chapter 29 - A Visit to Gaius (1 BC)

Tiberius took matters into his own hands. In order to refute charges that he was planning a military uprising, he discontinued his training exercises on foot and horseback at the parade grounds. He stopped wearing his army uniform, and even the toga, and dressed completely in Greek cloaks and slippers.

Then he decided to visit Gaius, who was staying on the island of Samos, three days' sail to the north. Perhaps he could end the rumors by assuring Gaius in person of his full support and obedience.

This gave Marcus Lollius an opportunity to punish his old enemy. When Tiberius arrived, Lollius detained him from seeing Gaius and instructed him in the proper way "for a Greek supplicant" to approach his Roman masters. "You may only have an audience with Gaius Caesar if you bend your knees."

Tiberius spun on his heel and began to leave, but pulled up short when some officers blocked his way. He saw in their wolfish grins the possibility that he could be arrested, even thrown at Gaius' feet as a would-be assassin. It seemed he had no choice but to go through whatever performance Lollius had planned for him.

Tiberius knew that Gaius was his best hope for a return to Rome. As a boy, Gaius had worshipped him and his brother Drusus as military heroes. Now, the main objection to a reprieve for Tiberius seemed to be his potential rivalry with Gaius and Lucius. If he could convince the young prince that he posed no threat, then Gaius might intercede on his behalf with Augustus.

Tiberius was "escorted" into a reception room with a raised dais at one end. Lollius stood in front of him and signaled for him to kneel. Tiberius complied. Then, in a grandiloquent voice, Lollius said. "As you have humbled yourself before me, your entreaty will be answered. You may see the noble Gaius Caesar!" There were smirks among the officers – Lollius had turned things around so that Tiberius was bowing to him!

When Gaius entered the room, he was immediately embarrassed to see a former consul and tribune of Rome in the position of a slave. He flushed red and motioned for Tiberius to rise.

It was clear that Gaius was confused. His instinct was to greet his former stepfather with respect and even affection. But he had been advised to be cautious and aloof. Lollius moved to his side and frequently whispered in his ear.

Gaius gestured for Tiberius to speak:

"Please accept my compliments, Caesar, and my wishes for your well-being and the success of your mission. It is good to see you again! You have grown into a splendid young man. Rome is fortunate to have such a protector."

"It is good to see you as well, Tiberius. You were also once Rome's protector, and a good one. It is a shame that you have sunk so low."

Tiberius was insulted. He shot back. "And that your mother has fallen into disgrace."

He immediately regretted the comment. Lollius whispered to Gaius, whose expression hardened, "What is it that you require of me?"

"Noble Gaius, I have come here to assure you of my loyalty, to you and to Augustus. There are rumors that I seek to regain my former status. They are completely untrue. I have begged your father to send someone to observe my behavior, which would soon put all suspicions to rest. I am retired now, Gaius. I have no political aspirations whatsoever."

Gaius was circumspect. "That may be true, Tiberius. I hope that it is true."

There was a long awkward silence. The audience was over. Tiberius turned to leave. Gaius watched him, hesitated; then abruptly invited him to dine with them. Tiberius agreed.

Eventually, as the wine flowed, the two men managed some civil conversation. Gaius asked for pointers in dealing with the Armenians and Parthians. Tiberius was pleased to be of service to Rome once again, even if only as an advisor. He realized that he missed high level diplomacy. He had been good at it, he believed.

He also realized that Gaius was ill-suited to his role. In many ways, he was like Tiberius – uncomfortable with public acclaim, overly serious and self-doubting. He felt a twinge of compassion for the boy. He hoped that Gaius felt some compassion for him, too.

"Gaius, I am a lost sheep on Rhodes. I yearn for Rome. I haven't seen my son in five years, nor my mother. Won't you speak on my behalf with Augustus? You needn't fear me. Augustus only raised me so high to hold your place until you were old enough. And now you are. There is no going back. I would not wish it, even if there were."

But Gaius knew Tiberius was far more qualified for his position than he was. And that he still had supporters, especially in the northern armies. Gaius was too insecure to let his boyhood idol return to the center of power. Even with Tiberius in obscurity on Rhodes, he felt threatened by him.

"Let me have a success or two first, Tiberius. I am still in your shadow."

Chapter 30 - Vipsania and Drusus (AD 1)

The following year, Vipsania's husband Gallus became the proconsular governor of the province of *Hispania Tarraconensis*, in northeastern Spain. Once again, he decided to take Vipsania with him - but with his mother to keep her in line. They would stay in the beautiful port city of Tarraco, on the Mediterranean coast.

Vipsania was able to bear the insult of Salonina's presence because Drusus would also accompany them. Perhaps time away from the capital would do him good.

Though Drusus had been in her household for two years now, Vipsania had yet to crack his shell. The impressions made by Julia and her set remained deep. He was obsessed with games and gladiators, and, as his younger half-siblings had discovered, he was a bully. Like his father, he had a hot temper and great physical strength. Too often, Drusus used his muscle to inflict pain.

Drusus also inherited Tiberius' athletic and military prowess and his general appearance. His facial features were heavier and blunter than his father's, however, and he would not be so tall. He was now 14 – the age at which it was customary for a Roman boy to don the *toga virilis*, the clothes and status of a man, and be presented in Roman society as a full citizen. This ritual was usually arranged by a boy's father. But Tiberius was not around.

Gallus' solution to the problem was for him to adopt Drusus - a move that would cement his connection to the imperial family. Vipsania was ambivalent about this. If Gallus adopted Drusus, then she could remain close to her son, even after he married. On the other hand, Tiberius would be mortally wounded to have Drusus taken away permanently. Her strategy was to postpone a decision by advising Gallus to consult with Livia on the matter. She knew that Gallus would hesitate to broach this subject with the empress, Drusus being her grandson. And so the boy's future remained uncertain.

Soon after they arrived in Tarraco, the new governor and his family attended a reception in the city's forum. One of the dignitaries, a rather rough looking man, congratulated Gallus on Drusus' (nonexistent) resemblance to him. An officer interceded and informed the man that Drusus was the son of Gallus' wife from an earlier marriage. However, Gallus winked at the man and said under his breath. "Let's just say I knew my wife before I married her."

The implication was clear. Vipsania overheard and was mortified. Later, she took Gallus to task for his insinuation. He responded, "I am trying to help the boy by freeing him from association with Tiberius. If you haven't noticed, your ex-husband is in disgrace. What can he do for Drusus, other than embarrass him? This is why I keep saying I should adopt the boy."

————

Suddenly, Thrasyllus began to lecture Alcinous on the evils of gladiatorial contests. "No doubt, there are noble gladiators whose behavior in the arena is exemplary. But the spectacle has a brutalizing effect, especially on the mob and on the young - boys like Drusus. He was a fanatic about the games his whole life. In later years, he was even nicknamed 'Castor' after a popular fighter. And you may have heard of the 'Drusian sword,' which was named for him? It's as sharp as a razor. When he was grown, Drusus even had Roman knights fight as gladiators - one of them was killed before Tiberius forbade the practice.

"Tiberius himself has always abhorred gladiatorial display. He limited the frequency of the games in Rome when he became emperor and would often ridicule Drusus for his obsession with them. Vipsania shared Tiberius' views on the subject. However, in an effort to understand her son better, she attended the arena with Drusus in Tarraco.

"As the governor's wife, she was able to sit close to the action. It disheartened her to see the blood lust in her son's eyes – his complete fascination with the spectacle and gore. But Vipsania gradually understood that the games were cathartic for him. His fears and resentments were somehow resolved through the brutal logic of combat. She knew that Drusus had been damaged – by the breakup of his family and the experiences he had in Julia's household, and especially by his father's abandonment of him."

————

It was a pleasant evening in Tarraco. The others had gone into the house, leaving Vipsania and Drusus to contemplate a moonrise over the Mediterranean. Soon they would return to Rome and Drusus needed to know what his future would be.

"Gallus wants to adopt me. I have no objection. I haven't seen my real father in years and I don't admire him. Besides, he can't help me with my career the way Gallus can. I could stay with you, and my brothers and sisters. I have decided to accept his offer."

Vipsania's thoughts turned to Tiberius, to their happiness when Drusus was a baby. Life would be simpler if Gallus adopted her son, but she had misgivings. Foremost among them was her loyalty to Tiberius. But there were other considerations.

Drusus was the one thing that she still shared openly with Tiberius – he was their child. And Gallus was not the sort of man she hoped Drusus would become. Tiberius was. She couldn't let go of the hope that they would be close someday, that Drusus would know his father as she knew him.

"Before you make this decision, you must have a better understanding of Tiberius. He is in an awkward situation now, it is true. But he is still a good man who has done many noble things. He may be great again some-day."

Drusus was exasperated, "Mother, we have nothing in common. You know I love the games, and the theater – he has contempt for them. He left Rome – I love Rome. It is my home, where all my friends are, where my future is. Right now, I don't have a father. I will need one if I am to get anywhere in life."

Vipsania placed her hand on his shoulder. "All I am saying is that you should understand your father before you reject him. Do you know why Tiberius dislikes the games? He believes that they spend blood needlessly. He has spent more human blood than any man alive – all for the sake of Rome. No one has taken greater pains to avoid the unnecessary loss of life than Tiberius. And yet lives are wasted in the arena, and to greater acclaim than was ever given to his soldiers, who died to protect us.

"And the theater? Tiberius has had to play a part his whole life. His role has been scripted by others, and he has been forced to bow and smile when his heart was broken. So he has no time for imaginary tragedies – his have been all too real. But it is more than that. You know how the actors ridicule him."

"He shouldn't be so sensitive. They make fun of Augustus, too, and he doesn't mind."

"It is more complicated than that, Drusus. Tiberius doesn't care what people think about him. He can take any sort of abuse if it is based on truth. But he has a very highly developed sense of justice. To be falsely accused, to be misrepresented – this is what rankles with him. He doesn't mind if people despise him as long as they despise him for the right reasons. The actors portray him as ambitious and disloyal, and a coward – and he is none of those things. But people believe it. Even you believe it."

Drusus was quiet. It would be easier for him not to understand his father.

Chapter 31 - Reprieve (AD 2)

Meanwhile, the cloud over Tiberius had been darkening. Word of his abasement at Gaius' headquarters spread rapidly. His detractors asked themselves, if he bows at the feet of Marcus Lollius, why should they fear him? Even on Rhodes, he was shunned and taunted. When he attended lectures, all of the good seats were already reserved. Men stood in his way at doorways or neglected to hear his greetings. The magistrates scrutinized his assets in a heavy-handed way, complaining that he had to be hiding something to avoid taxes.

Alarming reports trickled in. The people of Nemausus (Nîmes) in Gaul had overturned his statues and busts. They saw Tiberius as a rival to the sons of Agrippa, their great benefactor. His statues were defaced or melted down in other cities as well. He had become a stock character in pantomime and farce, in Rome and elsewhere – the new 'Colossus of Rhodes,' also fallen into ruin. It seemed that the whole empire was laughing at him.

A story circulated that a guest at a dinner party given by Gaius offered to go to Rhodes and "fetch back 'the Exile's' head," a gift that his host refused. This reminded Tiberius of Ptolemy's unwelcome offering to Julius Caesar – the head of Pompey the Great. When would someone strike Tiberius first and ask questions later?

He often retreated to his boulder on the hillside and contemplated his predicament. Sometimes he would tremble with a blend of anger and fear. He looked at the watery horizon, wondering if the means of his death had already set sail.

And he thought of his son. The time had come for him to enter public life. Who would stand up for him? Gallus? The idea soured his wine. Tiberius missed Drusus. He regretted bitterly that he had abandoned him to pursue a hopeless dream.

He wrote urgently and often to his mother, begging her to press Augustus for a reprieve. His life might depend on it. Livia was finally able to soften her husband's feelings, because of Julia's role in his retirement and the plight of young Drusus. But Augustus was adamant that the decision belonged to Gaius:

"I will not seem to undermine Gaius' position, Livia - you know how insecure he is. Tell your son to address his entreaties to him and only to him."

"But he already has, and Gaius refused him."

"Then he has his answer. I will not overrule Gaius in this matter."

So Tiberius sent regular messages to Gaius, offering his services as an advisor on eastern matters, pledging his loyalty, and begging his permission to return to his family in Rome. For nearly two years, there was no reply.

———

Thrasyllus looked meaningfully at Alcinous and pointed heavenward. "Finally, as I had predicted, the stars began to favor Tiberius. Gaius was informed by the Parthian king that Marcus Lollius had been selling his influence to the eastern client kings. The charge was proven to be true and Tiberius' enemy was cast out of the prince's circle. Within a few months, Lollius was dead. He was replaced by Sulpicius Quirinius, an experienced and fair-minded man who had served with Tiberius in the Alpine campaigns.

"Quirinius was an admirer of Tiberius and he worked to reassure Gaius about his former commander. In his heart, Gaius was an admirer of Tiberius, too, so he finally relented. He wrote Augustus and told him that he would allow Tiberius to return to Rome on the condition 'that he neither seeks public office nor returns to military life.'

"And so the ship bearing news of Tiberius' reprieve finally arrived. After 7 years of voluntary - and then involuntary - exile, he was going home. He truly believed that his life as a statesman and soldier was behind him. Now he could live quietly, with his studies and his family. Perhaps the ordeal of Rhodes had been worth it after all?"

Chapter 32 – Another Birthday (16 November, AD 36)

It was a holiday. The island had filled up with visitors, bearing gifts and fulsome praise in honor of Tiberius' 77th birthday.

The annual festival of Jupiter was already in full swing. It was a custom on Capri to combine the celebrations, recognizing Tiberius as the earthly embodiment of Jupiter's wisdom and power. This was implied rather than stated, however – Tiberius would not let himself be called a god.

Among the visitors was the 17 year-old Tiberius Gemellus, the surviving twin son of Tiberius' son Drusus and his wife Livilla. Tiberius had some doubts about the true identity of Gemellus' father; Livilla had been having a torrid affair when the boy was conceived. But Gemellus was a pleasant lad, and the fact that Drusus never doubted his paternity meant that he *could* be of the emperor's blood.

Tiberius was perplexed about his grandson's future. Gemellus was old enough to be his heir, but not old enough to rule the empire. Also, public and military sentiment overwhelmingly favored Caligula to succeed because he was the son of the popular Germanicus, Tiberius' deceased nephew. However, Tiberius did not want to dispossess Gemellus entirely.

The emperor's solution had been to announce that both Gemellus and Caligula would be his legal heirs, but to say nothing about the transference of political power. He had held Gemellus back from public advancement, even from initiation into manhood, in the hope that Caligula would see him as a protégé rather than a rival, at least until he had a son of his own. If Tiberius defied the stars and lived many more years, events might allow him to change what now seemed inevitable – that Caligula would be the next emperor and Gemellus would be killed by him.

Gemellus had little interest in politics. He was more concerned with coming to terms with his personal history. His father had been poisoned by his mother when he was not quite four. And his mother had been starved to death by his grandmother when he was 12.

It was his father who interested him most of all. What sort of man was he? Gemellus hoped that his grandfather could fill in some of the blanks.

"What was my father like?"

Tiberius bowed close to his grandson and looked him in the eye. "Your father was a great man. Surely you've seen the monuments to him, the lists of his victories?"

"Yes. But all they tell me is that, like the Scipios, like Pompey and Julius Caesar, like Germanicus, he was a successful general. I want to know what made him different from other men; what made him unique."

Tiberius closed his eyes and remembered his son. "He was more business-like than Germanicus. He did what needed to be done without a lot of theatrics. He was relentless in the pursuit of his pleasures as well as his duties. He had gusto – never did anything half-way.

"He and I were very different, but his life was much like mine, now that I think about it. I believe he adjusted better than I did. He didn't rebel against his responsibilities or try to hide from them.

"I often ridiculed him for his extravagance – his lavish banquets and drinking bouts, his obsession with actors and gladiators. But he knew how to enjoy life as what he was – a Roman prince. I could never do that. I was always trying to be something else.

"He was like his mother Vipsania in that way. He accepted his fate without rancor, and he made the most of it. He didn't brood or feel sorry for himself. And he had many hardships - being torn from his mother when he was a baby, being abandoned by me when he was eight.

"I was not a good father to him. I came back into his life late and did not always support him when I should have. But I loved him, and I think he knew that, eventually."

Gemellus put his arm on Tiberius' shoulder. "I am sure that he of all people understood what you had been through. Why you did what you did. As you say, his life was much like yours."

Tiberius considered his grandson. He was a forgiving, warm-hearted boy. Gemellus must have been Vipsania's grandson after all.

Chapter 33 - Homecoming

The following afternoon, Thrasyllus resumed his tale: "Tiberius returned to Italy with only a couple of servants, and with Longus and myself, of course. We were greeted by Marinus and Flaccus in Ostia and made our way to the capital by cart.

"As soon as the city walls were in view, Tiberius jumped from the cart and ran ahead of us. He traced his fingers over the tombs and monuments along the way, through the leaves of the overhanging trees, over the grass and weeds by the roadside. When he walked through the gate, he fell flat on his face and kissed the earth. It was very moving to watch – a child of Rome had come home!

"Coming from a great city like Alexandria, I wasn't overwhelmed by Rome at first, but I was impressed by the activity of the people, the vibrant atmosphere. Alexandria is a sleepy town in comparison, Alcinous. Have you ever been to Rome?"

Alcinous shook his head. "You must see it someday. There are fountains everywhere, most of them the work of Agrippa. And when I saw the forums of Julius Caesar and Augustus, with their colonnades and magnificent paintings, and the temples of Venus and Mars, the theaters of Pompey and Marcellus, the sprawling Circus Maximus - I knew I was in the greatest city in the world.

"'Rome has changed,' Tiberius assured me then. New buildings had sprung up, and old ones had grown marble skins and sprouted ornaments of bronze and gold. And, of course, statues of Gaius and Lucius were everywhere. But Tiberius made no comment about them. He was obviously thrilled to be home.

"He did not go home, however. He moved into a modest dwelling on the Esquiline Hill near the gardens of Augustus' friend, Maecenas. His new residence was far away from the political center of the city – a more appropriate address for a life of retirement and obscurity. And I suppose he dreaded the memories that haunted his old house, both good and bad."

———

When Tiberius entered Livia's room, he was not prepared for the wave of emotion that engulfed him. Their correspondence had been regular, but practical in nature. As Tiberius had no father, Livia was an advisor to him; even a disciplinarian. But now she was only a mother, overjoyed to be reunited with her son.

He was deeply touched by her affection – she buried his face in her bosom and kissed his fingertips. Tiberius was moved to tears. He realized that, through all his trials and travels, she had been protecting him. And that he had missed her more than he knew.

They strolled together into Augustus' chamber. It was a shock. The emperor had aged terribly – his hair was white and his body had thickened. Everything about him was less vigorous than before. He was friendly to Tiberius, but there was something artificial in his conversation, as if Tiberius was an athlete who had lost an arm or a leg.

Finally, the small talk led to more important matters – Drusus' manhood ceremony, the conditions of Tiberius' return to Rome. Augustus tried to offset his warnings against any public role with a cheerier note.

"My dear Tiberius, you must remarry! You know it is against the law for you to remain single. There are penalties. Drusus still needs a mother. You can start a new family. We must set an example for society."

Tiberius had been agreeable and docile so far, but now his words were firm. "I will never marry again. Never! There was only one woman for me, and you took her away."

Augustus began to react, but Tiberius cut him off. "No. That is the past. I have not come home to dwell on the past. I have a son who needs me. I will live for him now."

Tiberius took a deep breath and continued. "But Drusus also has a mother. He lives with her. If I am going to be a true father to him, I will need to see her. Do I have your permission?"

"Vipsania? Yes, now that you are divorced from Julia, I have no objection."

Tiberius exhaled audibly.

"But don't think of rekindling the flame, Tiberius. She is married to an important man and I will not tolerate adultery, by anyone."

"No. I only want to consult with her about our son's career and marriage."

Augustus put his hand on Tiberius' shoulder. "I want you to know that the problems we have had will not reflect on your son. I have great hopes for his future; he comes from good stock."

Chapter 34 - He's My Son

Thrasyllus poked at a pebble with his cane, searching for the right words. "Alcinous, you have to understand the situation Tiberius was in. When he left for Rhodes, he was at the peak of his career. His powers almost equaled those of Augustus himself. He was the most feared military commander in the world. But now he was less than an ordinary citizen, unable to run for office or do any of the things he knew how to do. Yes, he always wanted a quiet life, but he also wanted to serve his country.

"His first order of business was to reclaim Drusus from the house of Gaius Asinius Gallus. Tiberius knew this would be a blow to Vipsania, but he could not let his son be raised and introduced to society by the little rodent.

"Twice, he sent messengers to Gallus' house to bring Drusus home – both times they were turned away. First with 'The Master is not at home,' and then 'Your Master will have to come himself.' Finally, Tiberius appeared at Gallus' doorstep in person. I was with him. We were shown into the *atrium*, but were kept waiting. At last, Vipsania appeared with Salonina and a pair of burly slaves."

———

Tiberius' eyes watered at the sight of Vipsania. She moved to a column for support. When she spoke, her voice was high and breathless. She was nervous, almost terrified: "Dear Tiberius, it is good to see you. I am glad you are back in Rome." Salonina nudged her elbow.

Tiberius looked at her intently, trying to read her thoughts. "I am happy to see you, too, Vipsania. You look well."

The words were formal, but they embraced with their eyes. Despite the awkward situation, neither could resist smiling.

And then Gallus burst into the room. He made a show of being busy with other matters, muttering to his assistant, looking over a scroll or two. Without looking at Tiberius, he finally spoke to him.

"So you have returned. Or come back to Rome, at least. What do you want from me?"

"My son!"

"So, now that I have raised and fed and protected him, you want him back, just like that?"

"Yes, just like that. He *is* my son, Gallus, despite what you would have people believe."

Gallus was taken aback – he didn't expect Tiberius to have heard about his innuendos. "And what of his mother? What of the boy's wishes?"

Tiberius frowned. No one spoke. Finally, Vipsania moved toward Gallus, her voice now stronger: "Drusus belongs with his father."

Salonina hissed. Gallus flared briefly, but she reminded him, "Livia will support Tiberius in this, my husband. So will Augustus."

Gallus backed down, gathered his scrolls and left the room. Salonina and the servants went with him. All at once, Vipsania was alone with Tiberius and Thrasyllus, who discreetly withdrew.

Vipsania and Tiberius shared a sigh of relief. He spoke softly and seriously to her.

"I regret taking Drusus away from you. You may see him as often as you wish, of course, but it is time for me to be a father to him."

"Yes, it is what I have hoped for, Tiberius. Let me take you to him." As they walked together through the house and into the courtyard, passing the frowns of servants and family members, they spoke nonchalantly, their hearts beating for every word.

"So, you have been a mother nine times now? Remarkable!"

"Ten, actually."

Tiberius was confused – Vipsania realized she had slipped. "No, you are right, nine..."

Tiberius seemed to understand. "You were thinking of the one we lost."

Vipsania could not let him know the truth. He would discover what Gallus had done to their child, what he had done to her.

"Yes, that must be it."

Chapter 35 - He's Not My Son!

For seven years, Tiberius had remembered Drusus as the little boy he left behind. He was ill-prepared for the reality of a 14 year-old raised by Julia, Gallus, and the worship of gladiators.

In turn, Drusus was unaccustomed to men like Tiberius, rooted in the old republican institutions and values. Tiberius despised ostentation, luxury, the games, the vulgar theater – all of which fascinated his son. Vipsania had spent her energies trying to refine Drusus' morality and education rather than his entertainments, but his father saw public tastes as indicators of character. He did not want his son to become a playboy.

Drusus was different from his father temperamentally. He was quicker to anger and he reveled in public attention. He shared Tiberius' fondness for wine – and for cucumbers - but in other ways, their tastes were quite dissimilar.

Drusus was the leader of his own gang of high-born ruffians, who spent their time terrorizing citizens, accosting women and boys, cheering too loudly for their favorite athletes. At the same age, Tiberius had been as studious and private as his son was outgoing.

———

The preparations for manhood proved beneficial for both of them. A father took his son through the daily rounds of a Roman citizen from his social class. In Drusus' case, this meant frequent visits to law courts, public meetings, and official ceremonies; to the forums, shops, and banks to witness the conduct of business; and to the outer halls of the senate house to eavesdrop on the proceedings. These forays into the heart of Roman life forced Tiberius to renew his old acquaintances.

Drusus was being introduced to a more sober side of life. He was overwhelmed by names as he met legions of his father's friends, clients, and business associates. "This is one of the most important parts of being a Roman citizen," his father pointed out, "remembering the names of everyone you meet."

Finally, Tiberius decided his son was ready to become a legal adult. Drusus exchanged his boy's toga for the *toga virilis*, the garment of manhood. In a solemn ritual, he shaved off his downy beard, placing the whiskers in a small silver urn for safekeeping.

A group of his father's most distinguished friends witnessed the ceremony. When it was complete, they made a procession to the local magistrate and Drusus' name was officially inscribed in the roll of Roman citizens, registering him in his father's voting district.

Tiberius found the whole process more evocative than he expected. He felt as if he himself was being re-enrolled as a Roman citizen after his years of exile. His thoughts often turned to his father, who died before Tiberius and his brother were ready to don their manly togas. He was grateful and proud that he had been able to fulfill this function for his son.

Drusus was torn by conflicting emotions. He was often glad to have his father's attention and support, and impressed by the deference and respect that many important people still showed to him. On the other hand, it seemed that Tiberius was trying to impose his old-fashioned values and manners on his son. He felt as if he was being poured into his father's mold.

The initiation ritual complete, Drusus thanked his father, but his first night as an adult proved that nothing had changed. He and his friends celebrated with a rampage - a tour of the brothels and taverns culminating in a rumble, in which a senator was injured. Drusus himself was taken into custody and released only when his identity was discovered. He arrived home bearing his cuts and bruises like so many wreaths and medals.

Chapter 36 - The Ends of Princes (AD 2-4)

Thrasyllus signaled the end of the day's lecture. However, as they make their way to the villa, the story continued. He was anxious to deliver Tiberius from his disgrace and get on with the story. And Thrasyllus knew that his time was short – he did not want to die with the tale unfinished!

He continued: "Soon after Drusus' manhood ceremony, the news of Lucius' death reached the capital. The younger of Augustus' two adopted sons had drowned in Massilia (Marseille) in southern Gaul, on his way to Spain.

"Augustus was devastated, needless to say, and Tiberius genuinely regretted the boy's passing. He even wrote a poem in honor of the lad: 'Lament on the Death of Lucius.' It was very well received at the time, though there *were* some who doubted its sincerity.

"The public reaction to Lucius' death was alarming. Many of the people demanded his mother Julia's recall from exile! The outcry was so great, in fact, that Augustus held a public meeting to hear grievances and explain his position.

"In the end, he compromised: Julia could not return to Rome, but she would be moved from her island of exile to Rhegium (Reggio), a pleasant city in southern Italy. Also, the conditions of her 'imprisonment' were relaxed. But Augustus was indignant. He said gravely to the crowd, 'If you ever bring this matter up again, I hope the gods will curse you with wives and daughters like Julia!'

"A year later, Augustus was struck by another even more powerful blow. Gaius was wounded in Armenia. An arrow found him during a siege - a marrow wound that would not heal. The young prince became depressed and listless; he even tried to retire from his office, as Tiberius had done. And then, on his way home to Italy, he died at the age of 23.

"Can you imagine the impact of this news? Think of Augustus' agony - two beloved grandsons lost in two years, and his plans for the succession completely demolished! He was 66 years old; who would succeed him now?

"The public was unnerved by the tragedy. Were the gods angry with Rome? What misfortune would fall upon them next? The streets filled with throngs of mourners, as frightened as they were aggrieved..."

Thrasyllus stopped abruptly at the imperial villa. "But, here, we have arrived for our meal. I will continue the story tomorrow."

This day's meal, however, was more like a counsel of war. News had arrived that the Aventine quarter of Rome was in flames! The fire had begun in the *Circus Maximus* and raged onto the densely populated Aventine Hill. Tiberius, despite his age, showed surprising mental vigor as he interrogated and instructed his officials. Macro, the praetorian prefect, had just arrived with reports of the destruction. Tiberius waved a bony finger at him as he gave his orders:

"All praetorian guardsmen are to assist in controlling the blaze and aiding the survivors. Imperial properties shall be opened for the use of displaced persons and food will be made available to them at my expense." He glanced at an official across the room, who nodded.

"I hereby appoint a committee, to be headed by four men of the imperial family, to assess the damage and to coordinate compensation and rebuilding efforts. I will make the sum of 100 million sesterces available from the imperial treasury for these purposes."

A gasp at the size of this sum was ignored by the emperor. The consul Sextus Papinius, who had accompanied Macro from Rome, spoke up. "Caesar, may I suggest that you add Publius Petronius to the committee. He has experience in assessing fire damage and will be of much use."

"Agreed," replied Tiberius, pointing at his secretary so that the change was recorded. He looked at Macro: "Let me make this very clear: anyone who attempts to profit from this disaster will be severely punished. I will be kept informed of all developments and will hold responsible anyone who is slow, inefficient, or corrupt in the performance of his duties. That includes every one of you. I will visit Rome early next year to inspect the rebuilding efforts." Another gasp, also ignored. "Now, regarding reconstruction of the *Circus Maximus*..."

Thrasyllus leaned toward Alcinous and whispered in his ear: "Not quite the demented old fool you thought he was?"

"Will he go to Rome?"

"No! Oh, he may start the journey, as he has done before, but he will turn back."

Thrasyllus explained: "When Tiberius left Rome 10 years ago, it was predicted that he would never return. I cannot disprove the prophecy, so Tiberius believes it, more or less. Sometimes, he tries not to believe, but he still wonders if getting too close to the capital will prove fatal, so he pulls up short.

"Just before you arrived here, he was in Tusculum, only 12 miles from the city gate. A few years ago, he sailed up the Tiber to the gardens of Caesar, within sight of the city. There have been many similar occasions. He always turns away.

"Also, he dreads the fuss he would raise in Rome. Everyone would want to see him, and he is more self-conscious than ever about his appearance."

Alcinous raised his eyebrows.

"Yes, I know I said he doesn't care what people think of him – but that is only if there is truth in it. He thinks that if people see him in his broken down condition, they will assume he is not fit to rule." Thrasyllus gestured toward the emperor, still energetically directing his officials. "Do you think he is fit to rule?"

Chapter 37 – Friends

As the fire relief proceedings dragged on, Thrasyllus wanted to resume the story. He led Alcinous to the lighthouse, which also served as an astrological observatory. It was a tower 80 feet high with an open deck on which a fire was kept burning, its light directed toward the sea by a screen of polished brass. Tiberius and Thrasyllus had formerly climbed it often to study the stars together. However, the steep staircase within the structure had become a challenge for both of them, and they only used it on nights of astrological importance.

Thrasyllus knew it would be deserted this evening, except for occasional visits by the caretakers to stoke the fire. He motioned for his student to grab a torch at the entrance. It was a long climb, with several stops along the way for Thrasyllus to rest. When they finally reached the top, there was a long pause while the old man regained his breath, and while Alcinous marveled at the view.

The story continued: "After Gaius' funeral, it began to dawn on people that Augustus had no choice – he had to reinstate Tiberius. The emperor was down to one grandson, an unpromising 15 year-old boy named Postumus - the last remaining son of Agrippa. There was also Germanicus, the very promising 18 year-old son of Tiberius' brother Drusus. But neither boy was old enough or wise enough to rule the Roman Empire. Only Tiberius had the experience, the qualifications, and the family credentials."

———

Among the first to realize this was Pollio, Vipsania's father-in-law. He was nearing 80 years of age and in ill health, but he retained his political acuity and ambition for his family. His instructions to Gallus were clear.

"Tiberius is the only possible successor right now, which is something we can turn to our advantage. But you will have to swallow a bit of your pride, my son."

"In what way?"

"If Tiberius takes the throne, Drusus' prospects will soar. Your sons are his brothers. You must strengthen this bond – and that means you must encourage Vipsania to see Tiberius as much as possible. Let her take your boys to visit Drusus; they will be her chaperones. But the closer she is to Tiberius, the better for our family. Do you see?'"

Gallus did see. When he instructed her, Vipsania was thrilled, frightened, and outraged all at once. She disliked being used in this way, and she would not seek favors from Tiberius. But the prospect of spending time with him and Drusus together...? She turned away from Gallus to hide her pleasure.

"You will go with our children, and you will remember that you are my wife!"

"Of course! I will not jeopardize the honor of the family. Tiberius and I are friends now, concerned only for the welfare of our son."

———

Thrasyllus shook his head slowly as he described the visits between Tiberius and Vipsania at this time. "As far as I know – and I was often present – nothing improper ever transpired between them during their time together. But there is no question that they savored every moment. Without a kiss or a touch, they became as close as they ever were. And all thanks to Pollio's ambition."

Chapter 38 – Decisions (AD 4)

Tiberius knew that Augustus would approach him at some point about the future. Now that Gaius was dead, he was needed to help govern. But pride kept the two men apart. As usual, it was left to Livia to bring them together.

The conversation did not begin well; Augustus took entirely the wrong tack: "Rome needs your services. I am willing to forgive your past indiscretions and restore you to full power. But you must take a solemn vow never to abandon your post again!"

Tiberius stiffened. "I am not inclined to give up my privacy. I feel too old for military campaigning. Besides, you have undermined my reputation for so many years - how can I expect to be taken seriously as a leader now?"

"How have I undermined you?"

"By refusing me leave to visit my family. You made me an exile, scorned and mocked throughout the empire."

"You made yourself an exile. There were reasons for refusing your return. Gaius needed a clear field." Augustus began to weep at the memory of his loss.

Tiberius rolled his eyes and began to leave. Livia stopped him. "We are here to discuss the future," she said, "not the past."

Tiberius was angry: "He's just like a woman. As soon as the discussion goes against him, he breaks into tears."

Livia raised her voice: "Then like a woman, he should be treated with respect and compassion!"

Tiberius gathered himself. "I do not believe in the principate. I do not want to be an emperor."

Augustus was suddenly composed: "You know what will happen when I die. Chaos and civil war! Who will take charge? Will you be his servant – or his victim? Perhaps it will be Asinius Gallus? He certainly wants the job."

Tiberius' back straightened. It was a low blow, but Augustus might have been right. Gallus was in as strong a position as anyone outside the imperial family. Tiberius began to feel trapped – was there no other way?

Augustus plunged the dagger further: "You fancy yourself an old fashioned Roman, don't you? A man like Scipio, or Cincinnatus, or your father. But what did you do? You retired in the prime of life – to study *philosophy*. You left your post because you were 'tired.' Rome needed you – she needs you now. Prove that you are a true son of Rome and not a self-centered "greekling!'"

Now *Tiberius* was in tears. He raged back, "What is a Roman without a family? Twice, you took away my family! First my mother, and then my wife! You broke my heart! Twice!"

Livia's hands covered her mouth. Augustus stumbled into a chair and began to weep again. Tiberius shook his head in disgust and turned to leave.

"No! Stop! You misunderstand!" shrieked Augustus. "I am not crying for me, I am crying for you. You are right. I am sorry. Forgive me!"

Tiberius knew that he meant it. Despite himself, he was touched. "Give me some time. I will think about it."

Thrasyllus interrupted the story. He walked to the edge of the tower and looked below him. Assured there was no one to hear, he continued: "Now, if Tiberius has a weakness, it is his inability to make a decision where his own welfare is concerned. His thoughts loop and cycle in his head as he weighs the various factors and options, each one leading inevitably to its opposite. He expects fate to intervene – when it doesn't, he is at a loss."

"This is why he looks for answers in the stars. It is why he has always needed a right hand man – to help him draw conclusions. But he could only trust one person to advise him on this matter. Only one person understood him well enough - and what being an emperor would do to him - and that was Vipsania. So he arranged for one of her visits."

———

Vipsania was already aware of his torment; she knew the pressure he was under. It was a relief to be able to speak with him about it.

"You know what is on my mind, Vipsania. I don't know if I can do it again."

She lowered her eyes. "Can you live with not doing it? Imagine yourself in the future, watching another man rule. Will he be threatened by you? Will he be threatened by Drusus? Will he let you both live?"

Tiberius paced in front of her, rubbing the corners of his mouth.

She continued: "But those are negative reasons; there are better ones. You believe that no man can be content who avoids his destiny. Is this not your destiny? Your whole life has prepared you for this – and the gods have prepared no one else. You are kind, you are just, you are capable. Rome is fortunate that the gods have chosen such a man.

Tiberius leaned forward and took her hand. "I cannot do it without you."

She smiled and whispered, "The more power you have, the more I will be able to see you."

Suddenly, the decision was an easy one.

Chapter 39 - The New Pupil

Thrasyllus paused at the sound of leather sandals scuffling up the light-house steps. There was a glow in the doorway, and then Tiberius appeared, aided by Caligula. Alcinous trembled slightly – to be at close quarters with the emperor was still terrifying.

Tiberius gestured towards the heavens. "What do the stars tell you, my old friend?"

"That I will die very soon."

"And when will *I* die? I wouldn't want to be here without you!" "You have another 10 years, Caesar, at least."

"But I don't want 10 more years!"

"Then you will have to move the stars!"

Tiberius laughed, "Or the earth."

Caligula added ambiguously, "Or find a new astrologer."

Thrasyllus had an impulse – why not let Tiberius himself continue the story? "I was just telling Alcinous about your career, after we came back from Rhodes and after the deaths of Gaius and Lucius. When you were asked to resume your duties."

Dealing with the fire in Rome had invigorated Tiberius – he was in the mood to talk. He looked at Alcinous for a moment and decided to reminisce.

"Well, I wasn't going to be a stand-in for Julia's family again. So I told Augustus, 'I will do it on one condition: you must adopt me as your own son.' That was the only way I could feel secure in my position.

"Augustus must have anticipated this because he didn't even blink. 'Of course, I will adopt you,' he said. 'But I have conditions of my own. You will be first in line, but I will also adopt my remaining grandson, Agrippa Postumus.'

"I was surprised. Postumus was a brute, not very bright, only 17 years old. Augustus explained.

"'Tiberius,' he said, 'you must understand that Postumus shares my blood, and that I have the blood of the divine Julius Caesar in my veins. The best way for us to avoid civil war is for there to be no question in the minds of the Roman people who the gods want to rule them. And who else but the sons and grandsons of a god?'"

Tiberius folded his arms. "Now, I'm a republican at heart. What he said disgusted me. But Augustus had given the empire three decades of peace and prosperity after a century of upheaval. How could I argue with him?

"And, of course, there were more conditions: 'For the same reason, I want you to adopt your nephew Germanicus ahead of your son Drusus. I want Germanicus to come after you in your family line.'"

Tiberius sighed. "Now, no matter what people say, I did like Germanicus." He turned to Caligula, Germanicus' son, and continued somewhat apologetically. "Yes, he was a bit annoying – much too cheerful for my taste. By Zeus, he would even smile when reporting a disaster! And he was too anxious to be popular, in my opinion. But he was competent, and he was a likeable fellow.

"However, I didn't see why he should take precedence over my own son. Again, Augustus explained: 'Germanicus is my sister's grandson and he will marry my granddaughter Agrippina. The bloodline of the divine Julius must take precedence, if age and competence are more or less equal.'

"What could I say to that? So I agreed and was formally adopted by Augustus. My name became 'Tiberius Julius Caesar.' I renounced my position as head of my own family and became the emperor's pupil, like a child in his house."

He laughed out loud. "Born again at the age of 45! But I was a dutiful son to him. I still am, isn't that so?" Caligula nodded vigorously.

"My first 'lessons' as Augustus' pupil were the pacification of Germany and Illyria. After all those years, I hadn't forgotten how to win victories. And the Illyrian war was the worst Rome had faced since the time of Hannibal. It lasted for three years. It was a bloody mess!"

"And you were honored for your victories with a triumph," observed Thrasyllus.

"Yes. Too much fuss for my taste, but Augustus was pleased. And before long he had had his fill of Postumus Agrippa and disinherited him. He imprisoned him on the tiny island of Planasia and I was the only one left - the chosen heir, whether I wanted to be or not. Under the circumstances, there was no choice."

Tiberius lost his train of thought in the stars. Meanwhile, Caligula frowned thoughtfully. He wondered, was he the 'only possible heir'? Or would Tiberius choose Gemellus, his 17 year-old grandson, to succeed him? Caligula, the son of Agrippina, had Augustus' blood in his veins. Was it now worth less than the blood of Tiberius?

Tiberius tapped him on the shoulder: "There's a chill in the air. I think I'll go soak a while in the *caldarium*." He and Caligula shuffled back down the stairway, leaving Alcinous and Thrasyllus alone. Alcinous was surprised his teacher wasn't invited to join the emperor in the baths.

"Are you cold, Master?"

"A little." He read Alcinous' thoughts. "Oh, he generally bathes alone, or with the children."

Again, he read Alcinous' thoughts. "It's not what you think. I don't believe anything more than splashing around and a little massage goes on."

Alcinous had heard that Tiberius pursued lewd sexual practices when bathing with the children, whom he called his "minnows.' Supposedly, he made them swim underwater and nibble at his private parts.

Thrasyllus was obviously a bit uncomfortable with this subject – he didn't really know what went on in the emperor's private baths, and he had heard the rumors, too.

"I don't believe that Tiberius is guilty of anything more than pretending to be young. Besides, what a man does with his slaves is his own business."

Alcinous persisted, "I heard that he has the 'minnows' thrown from the cliff when he is done with them. Is that true?"

"Absolutely not! Don't you think I would know? Many men have been thrown from the cliff, but for good reasons. Why would a man throw away his own property? Even a man as wealthy as Tiberius?"

Chapter 40 - Back in Her Life (AD 4-14)

These were happy times for Vipsania; Tiberius was a busy man, but when he was in Rome, there were no obstacles to their seeing each other. Also, to her relief, Gallus had stopped visiting her room when her child-bearing came to an end. She was now in her late 30's, busy with the education and betrothal of nine children.

The year after Tiberius returned from Rhodes, her father-in-law Pollio had died at the age of 80. Though Vipsania had come to love the old man, his resentment of her connections had encouraged the rest of the family to mock her. Now they were less bold. Salonina, in fact, retired into her grief and seemed to forget all about her daughter-in-law.

Ever since leaving Ephesos, Vipsania had corresponded with the high priestess Artemis. The two women had no secrets between them. Vipsania wrote:

"...My home life has become much more bearable. My connection with Tiberius promises rapid advancement and high offices for all my sons, so I am treated with greater respect than before by Gallus and his mother...

"...Drusus is showing some signs of maturity, due largely to his new responsibilities as a magistrate. His vices remain strong, but they do not interfere with his duties. I am confident that marriage and family life will settle him down further.

"The choice of his bride is not entirely up to me. The union will have dynastic implications, so I have consulted with Livia and Antonia. When I was married to Tiberius, they were my mother-in-law and sister-in-law, and I love them both dearly. Conferring with them reminds me of earlier days and I feel that I have been restored to my former life and position.

"Our choice for Drusus is Antonia's daughter Livilla, the widow of Gaius and sister of Germanicus. It is the best match for him politically.

"However, I must confess that I have misgivings. It is true that Drusus and Germanicus are the best of friends, and that will be an advantage. But there is something about Livilla that disturbs me.

"When she was a small girl, Livilla was not attractive, either in personality or in appearance. She was teased mercilessly by the other children.

To everyone's surprise, she blossomed into a great beauty, very like her mother Antonia. But the scars of her tormented youth - her early marriage to a man whom she seldom saw and widowhood at age 16 - are clear to me. She is distrustful and insecure, and she uses her beauty to manipulate people.

"Drusus is spellbound by her charms, of course, and there is no political alternative to the match. But I am concerned..."

Artemis' next letter to Vipsania arrived:

"My dear friend, I have a story to tell that will delight and amaze you! Some months ago, a high priestess from a temple of Artemis-Persephone named Melissa came to pay her respects to my goddess. She is a good woman, gentle and discreet. Shall I tell you where her temple is located? No place other than *Sardis!*

"I thought so highly of this woman that I took a chance, for which I believe you will forgive me. I asked her to inquire in her city about a young girl, adopted at such and such a time, wearing such and such a talisman. I did not tell her on whose behalf I asked this favor.

"I believe you will be overjoyed to know that her search was successful! Your daughter flourishes! Her name is Helena, the daughter of Telemachos. He is, by all accounts, a good man and well-situated. He is a landowner with large flocks of sheep - I know that will please you. I am told that Helena is very tall and already beautiful, and that she is teased by the other children that her parents must have been gods.

"Neither Helena nor her family is aware that inquiries were made about them – their story was known by one of my friend's acolytes, who she says is completely reliable..."

Vipsania shivered with joy as she read this. There was an overpowering impulse to run and share the news with Tiberius. She clung to her senses and the door frame to keep herself from going.

Chapter 41 – The Earth Moves (AD 14)

Tiberius stood off to the side of a third floor balcony with a panoramic view of the Roman Forum. He could not see the people below, but he heard their voices. Like ocean waves, their groans of sorrow and fear mingled and washed over him. Augustus was dead!

Thrasyllus waited for the words to sink into Alcinous. Then he continued.

"By this time, Tiberius had been emperor in all but name for several years. He had all the necessary powers to rule, but he lacked Augustus' personal popularity. There was a sense of foreboding in Rome. Tiberius took it personally."

Alcinous reacted. "I don't see why he took it that way. Certainly the people were afraid of the unknown, not Tiberius?"

"Yes, but you must remember – Tiberius was always the second choice. The people preferred his brother Drusus, and then Gaius and Lucius. They sided with Julia when they separated. After he became emperor, they preferred Germanicus.

"Even now, there are many who wait for Tiberius to die so Caligula can take over. The Jewish prince Herod Agrippa is in jail at this very moment because he was overheard telling Caligula he wished the 'old goat' would die so he could succeed him. And there have been many plots and conspiracies.

"Tiberius has done more for Rome than any of his rivals, and he is respected by many. But he is loved by very few."

———

While Tiberius was listening to the city mourn and tremble over the death of Augustus, the co-prefect of the praetorian guard entered the room. His name was Lucius Aelius Sejanus, a knight who had served under Gaius in the East and then rose to prominence with his father, the senior prefect. Tiberius was already relying heavily on Sejanus and counted him among his closest friends and advisors.

At Tiberius' request, Sejanus had summoned Gallus. And Gallus brought his shadow, Syriacus - the very man who had noticed Vipsania's pregnancy in Ephesos 18 years before.

Tiberius didn't like Syriacus, but for superficial reasons. He had an enormous curly-topped head that wobbled aimlessly on his soft, short-limbed body. His movements were gradual, like the oozing of fish sauce, but his thoughts and words darted and flashed. Tiberius glared at Syriacus until he slowly withdrew. Sejanus left with him, leaving Tiberius and Gallus alone.

Gallus delivered the expected platitudes about Tiberius' personal loss and the assurances of loyalty and support. Tiberius was genuinely aggrieved by Augustus' death – he had become more like a father than he ever expected – but Gallus was not the man he would share his feelings with. So he got straight to the point.

"I ask you to relinquish Vipsania."

Gallus sighed loudly, "So, you will be *that* kind of emperor, will you?"

Tiberius struggled to remain calm. "I am asking, Gallus, not demanding. I need an empress. She is the daughter of Marcus Agrippa – it is her birthright. I cannot do what I have to do without her support."

"But you have Livia."

"My mother is an old woman. I need a wife by my side."

"If you are truly 'asking,' then my answer is 'no.' Do you think I will give up the mother of my sons? You made a choice when you divorced her, Tiberius. It seems to be turning out rather well for you. That should be enough.'"

Tiberius frowned. "You know that I have no desire to rule. But destiny has put me in this position. It is my intention to restore the senate to its rightful place at the center of power."

Gallus frowned. "If you do not want to be emperor, there are others who do!"

Tiberius roared back: "And I suppose you are among them?" Gallus realized he was on dangerous ground and retreated.

Tiberius was exasperated. "I shouldn't have to ask this."

"No, you could do to me what Augustus did to your father, what he did to you."

Tiberius winced. "But Gallus, you don't love Vipsania!"

Gallus scoffed: "Did you love Julia? This isn't about love, Tiberius. I didn't marry Vipsania for love. I married her so that I would be connected to the imperial family. If I gave her back to you, I would have nothing."

"Your sons' mother would be an empress! That is something."

"Then they would be her sons and not mine. And what would I be? A laughing stock. A man without a family! Be warned, Tiberius, if she divorces me, she will lose our children, my children. She will be a stranger to them, I will see to that."

The meeting was over. Gallus rejoined Syriacus and the two men left the building. Gallus glanced over the reason he was summoned – his mind was on larger matters.

"The fool, he wants the senate to rule. The shepherd wants the sheep to tend his flocks for him! Well, I won't have it! I didn't marry his ex-wife so I could be connected to a figurehead!"

Chapter 42 - The Story Ends

Thrasyllus explained: "Tiberius was determined from the beginning of his reign to restore the republic. He would return to the senate the powers that Augustus had used for good before an unworthy Caesar could use them for ill. This was his mission.

"But he knew the transition of power would take time; that he would have to cajole the senators, give them responsibilities gradually. And that he would have to rule until they were ready.

"However, despite his good intentions, Tiberius was not the man to lead a revolution. He was not a great persuader like Augustus; his speeches were long and intricate, full of subtlety and obscure allusions. The longer he spoke, the less he was understood, and he generally spoke at length. He could inspire soldiers to great deeds in battle, but not a gaggle of corrupt and jaded senators.

"Besides, after 44 years of Augustus' rule, Romans had become accustomed to an emperor. And there were many men like Gallus who did not want the return of the republic for their own selfish reasons. These men would seek absolute power for themselves if Tiberius stepped aside. Or they would turn to other members of the imperial family."

When Thrasyllus and Alcinous returned to the imperial villa, they heard the news. A phoenix, a supernatural bird that lives for centuries, immolates itself, and is reborn from its own ashes, had been spotted in Egypt! It could only mean the dawn of a new age.

For many, this was a sign that Tiberius would die very soon, but it had another, more personal meaning for Thrasyllus. It proved his calculations that his own death was imminent. "A week from today," he said to himself.

He had long known that his time was coming. His affairs were in order. Everything was done except finishing the story. He had to complete it or the secrets would die with the emperor. And, despite what he had been saying, he knew that Tiberius would also die soon.

"No one will ever understand his reign, what he has done, unless they know," he thought out loud. He resolved to spend the last of his days and energies telling Alcinous the truth.

That evening, in his home with his wife Aka, Thrasyllus suffered a paralyzing stroke. He lost the ability to speak and the use of the right side of his body.

Alcinous visited him over the next few days, but there was no recognition in his teacher's eyes, no sign of recovery. Seven days after the seizure, he died.

Aka told Alcinous that Thrasyllus had predicted the exact day and hour of his passing. Alcinous realized why he was in such a hurry to complete his tale. He had believed he had enough time, but he never imagined how he would spend his final days.

Alcinous was bewildered. His mind was filled with what he has been told, but he was overwhelmed with questions. "Did Tiberius and Vipsania ever renew their love? Did their daughter in Asia survive and learn who her parents were? How did all of this have anything to do with his conduct as emperor?"

After the funeral was over, he made arrangements to leave the island. It was too late in the season for a safe passage by sea to Alexandria, so he would spend the winter in Italy. Thrasyllus told him he should visit Rome, now he would.

As he sat on board the ship that would take him to the mainland, his gaze climbed the cliffs beneath Tiberius' villa. Alcinous was grateful that he witnessed none of the perversions or cruelties that he expected on Capri. He had learned that Tiberius was not the monster that people said. But he was still an enigma. Perhaps the rest of the story would have made him less of one.

There was a commotion at the far end of the ship - it had been boarded by a pair of praetorian guardsmen in full uniform. They barked a few questions at the captain and clomped rapidly in Alcinous' direction. He felt himself go pale and break into a sweat. He thought of jumping overboard, but his limbs wouldn't move. Finally one of the soldiers spoke to him, much too loudly.

"Are you Alcinous, the student of Thrasyllus?"

Alcinous' bowels quaked. "Yes, sir. I am."

"Come with us. Bring your baggage."

Alcinous was taken to Tiberius' villa and made to climb a series of ramps and stairways, finally leading to a small room remote from the main part of the building. The room was decorated with fine bronzes and murals and has a large window overlooking the sea. There was no one there but the emperor, reclining on a couch in the corner, a flask of wine on a table beside him.

Tiberius motioned for the guards to withdraw. He smiled at Alcinous, "So, you were leaving us?"

Alcinous was terrified, and it showed. He stammered.

"Do not be afraid, Alcinous. If I wanted to harm you, I wouldn't have sent the guards away."

He leaned forward and spoke earnestly. "I know what Thrasyllus has been telling you. I know everything that goes on here."

Alcinous trembled.

"It's all right. I let him continue. He was right; someone should know what really happened."

Alcinous sighed with relief, a bit too loudly, he feared. "How far did he get? What did he tell you?"

Alcinous struggled to arrange his thoughts. "He told me of your happiness with Vipsania, and your divorce; of your retirement to Rhodes and your struggles to return to Rome."

He looked behind him, to make certain they were alone. "He told me why you went to Rhodes, of your visits to Ephesos, of Vipsania's child. Of Augustus' death and your plans to restore the republic."

"Where did he leave you?"

"He was about to describe your dealings with the senate, your plans to restore its powers."

"The senate? Ha!! The senate couldn't govern itself, let alone the empire!"

Tiberius rose to his feet. "I will tell you about the senate, but not today.

First I will correct the impression you must have of Vipsania."

Alcinous was surprised. "My impression is very favorable!"

Tiberius shook his head vigorously. "How could Thrasyllus understand Vipsania and what she meant to me? Greeks don't appreciate women the way we Romans do. It's true that you Egyptian Greeks have an inkling, with your almighty queens. But the Greek mind works differently than ours. You save your romantic illusions for boys."

"We make women our equals, or even more than that. Everyone knows about Antony and Cleopatra. But Augustus also was ruled by Livia, Germanicus by Agrippina. And I was ruled by Vipsania. She was a benevolent queen – a kind and gentle despot. I needed that; my wounds were deep.

"By Venus, how I loved her!" His eyes were watering. "She defined what a woman is for me – and no one has ever rewritten that scroll. Her body fascinated me. Her tender eyes, her smooth, lustrous skin, the wispy curls at the nape of her neck. Her nipples were the color of dates, and just as sweet..."

Alcinous the scholar blushed. Tiberius laughed out loud.

"I was once inhibited, too, you know. But power and Capri have made me bolder. Why should I care what people think? You will have to put up with it, Alcinous. It is time for me to remember, before I pass away. You see, I know that I will die soon. Thrasyllus taught me too well; I can read the signs as well as he."

He walked to the window and scanned the horizon. "Meet me here in the evenings, after we have dined. I will bring the wine."

Alcinous understood it was time to leave. He marveled at the difference between the storytellers. Thrasyllus had been delivering lectures; Tiberius was indulging himself, remembering for his own pleasure. More than that, he was the story as well as its teller. This would be fascinating!

Chapter 43 - Which Part of the Empire? (AD 14)

It was some weeks after Augustus' death when the senate convened to confirm Tiberius as the successor. This was a formality – Tiberius had held powers equal to those of Augustus for a year. He did not need the senators' endorsement to rule, but this would be a confirmation of his sole leadership, and of the senate's loyalty to him.

For Tiberius, it was much more than that. It was the opportunity to begin the rehabilitation of the senate as the governing body of the empire. He knew that he walked a razor's edge. If he abandoned his powers too quickly, ambitious men would see this as weakness and seek to replace him; if he accepted Augustus' powers too readily, the senate would remain complacent and ineffectual.

His strategy was complex. First, he would refuse to be emperor. This would alarm the senators and they would beg him to reconsider. It didn't matter if they were sincere or not – if he accepted power, it would be reluctantly and at their insistence. Therefore, he would be able to negotiate with them, demanding that they accept more responsibility. Together, they would develop a plan for sharing power. Whatever arrangement was made would be a consensus, arrived at by the senators themselves. The process of their rehabilitation would have begun.

——

It was a majestic scene in the *curia*, the senate house: 300 of its members in blinding white, purple-striped togas, arrayed in a gleaming marble room with fixtures of gold and a mosaic floor. In recent decades, the senators had raised acclamation and approval to an art form, as they demonstrated when Tiberius entered the chamber and took his seat of honor. He studied their expectant faces: it occurred to him that the more impotent they became, the grander they appeared.

He began with a glowing eulogy of Augustus: a remembrance of his services to the senate and people of Rome, and to Tiberius personally.

When he was finished, a senator rose to his feet and said: "Hail Tiberius Caesar Augustus, worthy son and successor of the divine Augustus Caesar!"

As one, the senators took to their feet and cheered. Tiberius squirmed and gestured for them to return to their seats. When they had, he astonished them.

"I refuse the title 'Augustus.' I cannot take my father's place."

The senators gasped in unison. "Augustus had divine powers of intellect. I am not his equal. I do not have his gifts or good fortune. I am 56 – a quarter century older than he was when he took control of the state. My eyesight is weak, I am weary from the wars.

"I have shared the anxieties of rule with Augustus for many years. I know that it is too burdensome for one man, unless that man is touched by the gods, as he was. I am not such a man. I do not want this awesome responsibility."

The senators were aghast. Without an emperor, there would be chaos - they had become dependent on the imperial bureaucracy and the emperor himself. And they wondered - could they trust Tiberius? Was this a ploy to weed out the disloyal senators? The ones who wanted a return to the republic – who or wanted to take his place?

They surged forward, shouting pleas to the gods, to Augustus, to Tiberius himself: "Do not abandon us, Caesar! We need your strength and wisdom! It is Augustus' will, it is divine will, for you to rule over us! We beseech you!"

Tiberius was pleased – this was precisely what he hoped would happen. He signaled to an attendant, who produced a scroll, written by Augustus himself. The senators listened as it was read aloud: a detailed description of the extent and resources of the Roman state, the number of citizens, subject peoples, the size of the army, the amount of taxes paid, annual expenses. It was overwhelming.

"Don't you see?" Tiberius continued. "No one man can administer so much. But, my brothers, look around you! We do not need to rely on one man! This chamber is full of men who can share the burden, as your ancestors once did. How much better-governed will the empire be when we work together!"

The senators erupted into even more urgent pleas for Tiberius to remain as emperor. But this is where Tiberius' strategy became too complicated. First, he would suggest that control of the empire be divided. The senators would realize how impractical that would be, so he would compromise and agree to what he wanted in the first place: that he would continue to rule, but with a greater involvement of the senate in all areas of government. Then, with time, he would be able to withdraw gradually until the republic had been fully restored.

Tiberius raised his hand for silence. "I understand your concerns, noble senators. I do not wish to abandon my duties as a Roman senator and the son of Augustus. I am, after all, your servant – the servant of Rome. But the task of government is too much for me. If you divide the job into parts, I will undertake the part that you assign to me. What will you take upon yourselves?"

The senators were stunned: divide the empire? Inconceivable! They muttered aimlessly, trying to discover what course of action was both safe and in their interests. But there was one man who understood what Tiberius was up to: Gaius Asinius Gallus.

He rose and walked calmly toward Tiberius. "And what part of the empire do you want, Caesar?" His eyes told Tiberius that there was a subtle allusion to Vipsania here. Then he turned to the crowd:

"Which legions shall be Caesar's? Which cities? How many ships? How many miles of road? Caesar must choose which part of the empire he will rule!"

Tiberius was in despair. By seeming to take the suggestion seriously, Gallus was ruining everything. Tiberius could neither choose nor withdraw the opportunity to choose.

He looked daggers at Gallus and said sarcastically: "How can the same man be the divider *and* the chooser?"

Gallus continued, "I only mean to demonstrate that it is impossible to divide the empire, Caesar. Power must remain in the hands of one suitable man. And who is more qualified, more deserving, to follow the noble Augustus, the savior of the entire world, than his son, the great and noble Tiberius? Two times consul, Triumphator, Imperator, Conqueror of the Alps,

Subduer of the Germans, Dalmatians, Illyrians..."

The senators rose in applause. They began to chant Tiberius' name. He had lost the moment. Gallus hurled an icy grin at him and returned to his seat.

Chapter 44 - King Saturn (December, AD 36)

She was the ugliest woman Alcinous had ever seen. She was tall and hairy, with a muscled torso and spindly arms and legs. She had a broad forbidding brow like the emperor's and enormous feet. She was Caligula! - in a short *chiton*, with a yellow wig and flowers in his hair!

Alcinous was stupefied. The prince scowled at him and explained: "It's *Saturnalia*, you fool! The Winter Solstice!"

The banquet hall was in riot: music, dancing, everyone in costume. Tiberius, dressed as a shepherd, was pouring wine for his servants, who sat at the table while their master waited on them.

When he saw Alcinous, the emperor raised both hands. "Here is our Lord and Master, King Saturn himself!" A golden crown was placed on Alcinous' head and he was shown to the seat of honor – Tiberius' place.

In the center of the table was a pile of brightly colored fleeces, each closed with ribbons and containing a gift. Tiberius himself distributed them, the first and largest to Alcinous. It contained an enormous cucumber with two cloth bags filled with coins tied to one end. The room exploded with laughter. Alcinous finally got it – it was a phallus!

"An auspicious gift for the coming year!" said Tiberius.

The next package was presented to Venus-Caligula. It contained a tiny gherkin, with tiny bags containing one coin each. Several guests laughed themselves onto the floor. Caligula accepted the joke and handled his gift in a lewd and suggestive manner. Then he sashayed seductively towards Alcinous. Tiberius jested, "Everyone! If you don't like your gifts, give them to Venus – she knows what to do with them!"

The rest opened their fleeces and mocked each other's cucumbers. There was the jingle of coins, the singing of songs, the drinking of wine. Great mounds of food disappeared.

Sometime later, confident that the party was a success, Tiberius gestured to Alcinous. They withdrew and made their way to the emperor's room. They were followed by an elderly servant, a man who had been with Tiberius since the days of Julia.

Tiberius turned to hear his slave, who offered up his coins. "Master, with this, I have enough money to buy my freedom! I have been saving for a long time – now I can do it!"

Tiberius put his arm on the old man's shoulder. "Save your money, my old friend. I will die soon and your freedom will be my gift."

The man was crestfallen. "Master, I do not want a reason to desire your death. Besides, I would rather purchase my freedom."

"I understand. You are free tonight in any case. This time, your Saturnalia will never end."

The man danced away in celebration as Tiberius and Alcinous entered the room.

The emperor was tired. He slumped to the couch. His grin had subsided into a weary frown. But then he began to chuckle.

"I remember the first *Saturnalia* after Augustus' death. I gave myself a very wicked present.

"At that time, I received letters of congratulation, condolences, promises of loyalty, reports of local matters from every city and province of the empire. I could not read them all, but I made a point of reading the one from Rhodes. I recognized the names of most of the magistrates who signed it.

"To my delight, they had omitted the customary prayers for the emperor's welfare at the end of the letter. A small detail, of course, but I remembered their mistreatment of me during my later years at Rhodes. I remembered their arrogance, their pleasure in my disgrace. So I summoned them all to Rome, without saying why."

———

Eurymachos could not tell whether his sickness came from fear or the tossing of the ship. Surely Tiberius had discovered his blackmail of Vipsania! He would be executed, but he would bring Marinus and Flaccus down with him, by Zeus! Whatever had possessed him to trust Romans?

Still, he wondered why so many Rhodian officials had been summoned along with him. Perhaps Tiberius wanted them all to witness his punishment? Or even to share it? Romans had been known to chastise a whole city for the crimes of one man.

When they arrived in Ostia, Eurymachos was somewhat encouraged to see that he was not treated differently than the others. They were all given comfortable quarters in the capital - he was not singled out in any way. But none of this calmed his nerves when they were brought before Tiberius.

The new emperor sat in his throne-like *curule* chair on a dais at one end of the room. He was silent while they groveled in his presence, trying to discern his mood and intentions. Outside, the city of Rome was in uproar with Saturnalian celebrations. Eurymachos wondered if his execution would be part of the festivities, perhaps after some ingenious tortures and humiliations.

Tiberius looked at him and clearly recognized him. He even nodded at him once, but without smiling. Finally, the emperor spoke.

"Noble fathers of Rhodes, I have summoned you here because of the letter you recently sent, informing me of the affairs of your great city. As you know, there are rules and customs regarding correspondence with the leaders of the Roman state. You have violated those rules by failing to conclude your report with wishes for my good fortune and continued health."

He suddenly stood up and his demeanor changed entirely – he became breezy and cordial. "You must know how superstitious I am. But not to worry – if you will follow me over here, I have arranged for all of you to correct the oversight."

There was a table on the far side of the room, with paper and pens for each of them. Tiberius explained: "I want each of you to write down the missing salutation in your own hand. Then you may go."

Like schoolboys handing in their lessons, the magistrates did as they had been told. Tiberius collected their papers as they left, one by one, accepting their bows as they backed away from him and hurried out of the room.

Tiberius laughed so hard at the memory that Alcinous worried he would injure himself.

Chapter 45 - The Slave Galley

The next evening, while the *Saturnalia* continued in other parts of the villa, Tiberius and Alcinous adjourned to the past.

"I promised I would tell you about the senate, and now I will. You will soon see why I gave up restoring the republic.

"The 'ship of state' had become a slave galley, and the senators refused to row unless I beat the drum. But I grew weary of drumming, so I let Sejanus beat it for me. History will blame me for that. That is just. He was a vicious man, though I thought he was my friend. He beat the drum only for himself. I suffered for my mistake, as did others.

"But I am getting ahead of the story. From the beginning, I relied on precedent. I took Augustus' words and deeds as my model and based my decisions on his policies. Augustus is my father and the deified father of Rome – it is my sacred duty to rule according to his wishes. I explained this to the senators. I had them swear allegiance to Augustus' acts, and I also bound myself to them publicly.

"Even after that disastrous first meeting, I hoped to stay in the background, to observe and let the senators take the initiative - even if they wouldn't make a move without my reassurance and approval. But Gallus would not allow it. He always forced me to act before I was ready, to declare myself, to take control.

"For example, there was a serious flood in Rome the year after Augustus died. I hoped the senators would deal with the emergency, but Gallus made a ridiculous proposal, designed to force me to intervene. He suggested that we consult the Sibylline Books, an ancient Roman collection of prophecies, for guidance about what to do.

"Well, no senator was going to scoff at this useless suggestion because the books are sacred. Consulting and interpreting them would take time – time that could not be spared. So I took control, rejected Gallus' proposal, and set up a committee to deal with the situation.

"Soon after, some actors and dancers caused a riot in Rome in which several people were killed. Some senators proposed that the instigators be flogged. Well, Augustus had expressly forbidden the corporal punishment of these entertainers; he enjoyed them and knew that their profession guaranteed they would offend people.

"As I hoped, the tribune Haterius spoke out in the senate, citing the decree of Augustus and vetoing the motion. But then that little rodent sprang to his feet and savaged Haterius, demanding that the senators override the veto. He was trying to force my hand once again; he knew that I would not allow a decree of Augustus to be overturned.

"However, this time, the senators actually sustained the veto without my involvement. I was encouraged. I shouldn't have been.

"The following year, I announced that I would leave Rome for a short while. My old friend Gnaeus Calpurnius Piso, knowing of my hopes that the senators would take responsibility, moved that they continue to conduct business during my absence. He said that this would 'enable them to understand their duties better.'

"I was very pleased by this, but, once again, Gallus took exception: 'This would be inconsistent with our national dignity! Any decision that we make will be suspect. Our decrees will not carry the prestige nor benefit from the wisdom of Caesar!'

"Again, I kept silent, hoping the senate would rise to the challenge. But the lazy devils sided with Gallus. Piso's motion was defeated and the senators adjourned until my return. 'Men fit for slavery,' is what I said – and I meant it!

"Gallus became even more aggressive, confident in his ability to manipulate the senators, as well as me. He introduced an insidious scheme that seemed to increase my powers, but in fact would tie my hands: 'I propose that Caesar be given the authority to choose political candidates and that they be elected to their offices five years in advance.'

"Well, this would have made me seem even more powerful, able to designate officials into the future. But, in practice, it would have removed my ability to reward and motivate people. Once a man's magistracy was assured, he had no reason to work hard or remain loyal to my policies! The measure was rejected - but Gallus had me fending off new powers rather than relieving myself of old ones.

"He was also behind many of the nauseating attempts by the senate to flatter me. It was proposed that the month of November, when I was born, be renamed 'Tiberius.' I asked them, 'But what will you do when there have been 13 Caesars?'"

Alcinous laughed out loud. Tiberius was in a serious mood, however, and took no notice.

"On another occasion, the senate tried to bestow an ovation on me when I returned to Rome after a short journey. An ovation is a great honor reserved for victorious Roman generals. I told them 'After winning many honors in my youth for genuine military achievements, I don't need to be rewarded for a successful tour of the suburbs!'

"But worst of all were the cases brought against men and women who had supposedly dishonored me or my family in trivial ways.

"Once, when my son was ill, a poet who was famous for his eulogy of Germanicus wrote one for Drusus. Drusus recovered, but the man was so proud of his work that he couldn't resist reading it aloud to a small but prestigious gathering. The senate, which was actually in session - even though I was out of town at the time - found the poet guilty of treason and black magic. He was promptly executed.

"I was furious when I found out about this, but what could I say? The senate had actually made a decision, even if it was the wrong one. I did arrange for a 10-day delay between future senatorial decrees and their implementation - so that I would have time to review them.

"On another occasion, in my own presence, a man named Granius was formally charged with three 'horrible' crimes: He had made fun of me; he had removed a head of Augustus from a statue and replaced it with my portrait; and he had placed a statue of himself on a higher pedestal than those of the Caesars. All of this was done in his own home, you understand!

"I lost my temper. Was my time and the senate's time to be wasted on nonsense like this? I stood up and roared sarcastically, 'Well, I will definitely want to vote on this very important matter! I will cast my vote openly and under oath, and I know that every man here will want to do exactly the same!'

"The idiots stared blankly at me. They didn't know if I was serious or not. Even my friend Piso didn't get it. He asked hesitantly, 'Shall you vote first then, Caesar, so that we will know how we should vote?'

"And these were the men that I hoped would rule the Roman Empire? The charges were dismissed at my request, but the senators still didn't catch on. Another man was charged with melting down my image in silver. I absolutely refused to hear that case, and, imagine this, I was criticized for not letting the senate consider the matter for itself!

"Do you see why I despaired of them? How could such a gathering govern the known world?"

Tiberius was red in the face by now. "But enough about the senate. I have remembered more than I wanted to."

Chapter 46 - The Earth Moves Again (AD 17)

It was late at night, but Helena was still awake, watching the stars from her front doorway. She heard thunder. She looked up at the cloudless sky. The rumbling grew louder and deeper and didn't cease. She realized that the ground was shaking. She could see the sheep in the moonlight, hurrying this way and that, not knowing where to go. Tiles slid from the rooftop above her. It was an earthquake!

She screamed and ran inside, scooped her two year-old from his bed and rushed outdoors as the house crumbled in her wake. Her mother was already outside, carrying a torch and a bewildered lamb. The noise was deafening and relentless; the baby screamed in Helena's arms, but could not be heard.

Fires sprang up everywhere as lamps broke and torches fell. Helena could see bits of landscape - rocking and swaying like the sea. The hills were like waves, rising as mountains, then sinking into ravines. The creek behind the garden spilled in all directions as its bed became a ridge. And still the thunder roared.

When it was finally over, she could hear the screams of the injured, and the silence of the dead. Every building had been flattened – barely two stones stood together in the whole village. The brush and buildings were in flames. Smoke and dust swirled over ruins and bodies. It was as if the Earth had collapsed into the Underworld.

Helena had lost her father, her husband, her home - and her bearings. In the light of day, she and her mother took the baby and stumbled into the ruins of Sardis, in search of food and shelter.

The story raced into Rome like a tidal wave: twelve cities in Asia had been destroyed. Damage had been done as far away as Sicily and southern Italy. It was the worst earthquake in human memory – tens of thousands were dead.

In Asia, the aftershocks rippled through the souls of the survivors. The whole empire trembled at the rage of the gods, wondering what would happen next.

Breathlessly, Vipsania read the list of ruined cities: Magnesia, Philadelphia, Cyme, Temnus, *Sardis, the hardest hit of all...* She was desperate. She hurried to the new palace in search of Tiberius. She found him inspecting the construction work.

He could see that she was distraught and steered her into an empty room. When they were alone, she sobbed uncontrollably. Tiberius was alarmed; had Gallus caused this? If so, he would rue the day! Finally, she was able to explain, but with an intensity that unnerved him.

"The earthquake...it is so horrible! You must promise me to help these poor people!"

"Of course, my dear! I have already engaged Marcus Aletus to lead the relief party. He will go to Asia with five lictors to assess the damage and coordinate the rebuilding. I will do all that is appropriate. You know that I will."

Vipsania nearly screamed at him, "No! You must do more than what is *appropriate!* You must do everything that can possibly be done, whatever the cost!"

Tiberius led Vipsania to a workman's bench and sat with her, his arm around her shoulder. Moved by the depth of her feeling, he said: "I will do all that is legally possible to relieve the stricken cities. And then I will do all that is personally possible, from my own funds. You have my word."

She knew that he did not understand, and that she could not explain it to him. So she lied: "It's just that, during my time in Asia, I made so many close friends and dear acquaintances. I can see their faces in my mind – their fear and devastation. I want to help them, but what can I do? Only you can help them!"

Tiberius had an idea. "Why don't you go with Aletus? You can see for yourself what is being done."

Propriety and habit urged Vipsania to say no, but she had to know that Helena was alive and safe. There was no other way. Tiberius could see that she was willing. "Take one of your sons with you - he can see to your comfort and safety."

Tiberius took pleasure in recalling his role in the relief efforts. "It was something that Vipsania and I did together – almost as if she were my empress. I would have been a much better ruler with her by my side. I know that.

"In the senate chamber, I outlined my program: an outright gift of 10 million sesterces to the city of Sardis and the remission for 5 full years of both senatorial and imperial taxes for all the cities seriously affected. The senators were stunned. Asia is the richest province in the empire; to forgive 5 years of taxes for the major cities was a stupendous sacrifice. One that the senators were loath to make.

"Gallus took the floor: 'Caesar is to be congratulated for his *extraordinary* generosity, but is this not excessive? The imperial treasury may be able to sustain such a loss, but the *aerarium*, the senatorial treasury, is not so prosperous.'

"I interrupted him. 'People are dying by the thousands from starvation and disease, Gallus. Their homes are nothing but rubble. Shall it be recorded that a former governor of the province argued against relieving their misery?' For once, Gallus was silent.

"I believe that the relief of Asia was the noblest thing I have done as emperor. The senate even issued a coin recognizing the 'restitution of the Asian cities.' Generally, I despise my coins; they display my worst feature - my profile, with my enormous nose. It is as if the Roman Empire is ruled by a flamingo! But this coin pleases me – my portrait is small, and it reminds me of Vipsania's compassion, of our working together.

"The people of Asia even erected a temple in Smyrna in honor of the senate, Livia, and myself because of our aid to the earthquake victims. I only allowed this because the senate was included – I still had faint hopes that they would live up to my expectations."

Chapter 47 – Sardis

The 42-mile journey to Sardis from the sea was a difficult one; the road was askew in many places, shifted horizontally or vertically by the quake. Vipsania frequently left her carriage and walked on foot.

She grew more anxious as they drew nearer, but also exhilarated – by the prospect of finally meeting her daughter, and by the breathtaking beauty of the mountain scenery. She had been virtually a prisoner the last time she was here, preoccupied with her own thoughts and fears. Now she came with her eyes and her heart wide open.

The road leading into the city swarmed with refugees living in goatskin tents and begging for help from the prosperous Romans. Coins wouldn't help these people; they needed food and shelter.

Vipsania advised Aletus to set up a center for the distribution of supplies near the temple of Artemis-Persephone. As they arrived, the splendid temple, the least damaged building in Sardis, stood majestically in the evening shadow of Mt. Tmolus. The mountain's towering dome symbolized the unshakeable goddess and was a beacon for the refugees. To the east were the supernatural stone spires of the city acropolis – towering gray cones piercing the azure sky. She wondered how a terrain so beautiful could be so deadly.

They were greeted by the local magistrates and temple staff. While enduring the formalities, Vipsania tried to pick out Melissa, the head priestess, the woman her friend Artemis has corresponded with. This woman knew of Helena and her family.

A slender, broad-faced priestess in a tiara finally emerged from the inner sanctum of the temple and moved to greet Vipsania personally. "Great lady, daughter of Marcus Agrippa, we are deeply honored by your presence. You have surely undergone many hardships to come here..."

Vipsania waved off her concern and described her plan of using the temple precinct as a base for assisting the victims. The priestess readily agreed. She explained the efforts that were already underway and told Vipsania what was needed most.

After the relief plans had been reviewed, Vipsania was shown to her quarters – one of the few residential rooms still standing. She took Melissa by the arm and protested.

"You are kind, but I have not come all this way to be a burden. Use this room for those who need it most. We have brought army tents with us, for ourselves as well as for the homeless."

"You are generous, my lady. This will inspire our people, to know that important Romans like you care so much."

Vipsania took Melissa's hand and pulled her aside. "There is something that you *can* do for me. I am looking for a young woman. Helena, the daughter of Telemachos. The high priestess of Ephesos wrote to you about her?"

"Yes, I know the woman. Her father and husband were killed by the quake."

"How awful! Was she injured? Is she safe?"

"She is unharmed. Artemis sent a messenger to me, begging me to find Helena and look after her. I found her among the refugees, with her mother and little boy. They are staying with us in the temple quarters."

Vipsania breathed completely for the first time in weeks. Her daughter was alive and close by. She had a son.

"May I see her?"

As she walked toward the reunion she had dreamt about for two decades, Vipsania drilled herself mentally: "Remember, she is my daughter, but she doesn't know that, she doesn't speak Latin, she has never been to Rome, she doesn't know who her father is – she may not even know she is a foundling."

However, as soon as she walked through the doorway, the secret was out. Helena's mother Chloe took one look at Vipsania – the image of her daughter – and knew. She covered her face with both hands. Helena, nursing her son on a couch by the wall, was mesmerized. She could not think; the apparition of a fine Roman lady, so alien and yet so familiar, had made time stand still.

"My name is Vipsania Agrippina. I am the wife of Gaius Asinius Gallus. He was the governor of Asia 21 years ago."

Chloe reeled and burst into loud sobs. She was terrified; she had lost her husband, her home – and now she would lose her daughter and grandson!

Vipsania rushed to her and kept her from falling. "Sister, do not be afraid! I will not take your daughter from you. How can I thank you for loving my child, for being a mother to her? Certainly not by taking her away!"

Chloe was calmer, but still frightened. Helena was overwhelmed. She knew that she had been adopted – one look in a mirror proved that. But she had no idea her mother was a Roman. Not to mention a wealthy one.

Vipsania spoke to her as she consoled Chloe. "You were wrapped in a green cloth, with a Trojan horse around your neck. It nearly killed me to let you go, but I had no choice. You were not my husband's child."

Helena barely moved. "I am Helena."

Chloe was now able to speak: "Because of the horse, we named her Helena."

Helena continued, very softly. "This is my son, Telemachos. After his grandfather." Her voice choked and her eyes glistened as she remembered their loss.

Vipsania walked Chloe to the couch and sat between the two women. She embraced her daughter – kissed her on the forehead for a long moment, then gazed at her in wonder. Her eyes were familiar, her hands, even her skin reminded Vipsania of her own when she was young.

Helena looked at her with the large brown eyes of a small child. "Who is my father?"

Vipsania hesitated. Then she produced a small silver coin, a *denarius*. Wordlessly, she placed it in Helena's palm and pointed at the portrait. Helena's eyes widened further. Vipsania put her finger to her lips. "Only one other person knows. No one else. Not even he."

"What sort of man is he?"

Vipsania measured her words. "In his heart, he is a kind man, a simple man, very gentle. He is under more pressure than you can imagine, than anyone can imagine. He is a peaceful man who has had to kill thousands of people; a family man who is alone; a sensitive man ridiculed by everyone; a private man forced to be a public icon."

Vipsania turned the coin over in Helena's hands to reveal a seated portrait of Livia. "His mother, your grandmother, is like him in that way - private by nature. But she has grown a hard shell to protect her from the world. Not your father – he is utterly defenseless, which sometimes makes him seem remote. But he would adore you."

Chloe lowered her head. Vipsania put her hand on hers and said. "No! She must stay in this beautiful place, far from Rome. I will help you rebuild, and give Helena a handsome dowry so that she can remarry and have more babies." She stroked her grandson's cheek. He smiled.

"Trust me, my dear. You do not want to be known as Tiberius' daughter. Your son would never be safe. High birth is what separated me from your father, and that is what separated me from you. It has broken our hearts so many times. Live the life that you know; it is far better."

Helena's mind was a torrent of thoughts. Only her nursing kept her from being overwhelmed by them. She briefly entertained the thought of an imperial destiny for her son, but Vipsania's words rang true. She was young, but she understood. She could see the pain of a public life in her mother's eyes.

Vipsania saw as much as she could of Helena, Chloe, and Telemachos during the three weeks of her stay in Sardis. But when she said goodbye, she knew it was forever.

Chapter 48 - Drusus and Germanicus

Tiberius rubbed his chin and looked at Alcinous. "Tell me, what is your opinion of Germanicus?"

Alcinous' smile answered for him. "I think he was a great man. I saw him once, in Alexandria, when I was a young boy. He was splendid, a blond Adonis, and his wife Agrippina was so tall and regal."

Tiberius frowned. "Yes, she was beautiful, in an equine sort of way. But she was a harpie; proud, stubborn. She never owned up to a mistake or issued an apology in her entire life. If not for her, Germanicus and I might have been friends. He was a good nephew, really, loyal and straightforward. A bit over-eager, maybe. But he was only her pawn.

"Agrippina believed that power belonged to her family by right – that I was an interloper who should have retired when her husband came of age. It didn't satisfy her that I gave him precedence over my own son, as Augustus had wished. She wanted me completely out of the way. So she did all she could to put Germanicus in the public eye and to encourage the people's preference for him.

"I knew this, but I still gave him his due: command of the armies in Germany; a triumph in Rome in the year of the earthquake; a consulship as my colleague the following year. But his reckless campaigns in Germany were bankrupting the state and achieving nothing of lasting value. So I transferred him to an important diplomatic role in the East and gave my son Drusus command on the northern frontier.

"Drusus and I were still squabbling at this time; I disapproved of his leisure activities. But he was an effective general – much more prudent than Germanicus – and their friendship helped to keep us all working together.

"Drusus was jealous of Sejanus, who was now my principle administrator and close friend. I needed someone in Rome to deal with the senate and Italian matters. That man couldn't be Drusus; he was needed in Germany. But he still resented Sejanus. The two even came to blows on one occasion."

Tiberius shook his head regretfully. "Looking back, I now realize that Drusus must have sensed that Sejanus was only seeking his own advancement; that he was not really my friend. He may also have had an inkling that Sejanus was having an affair with his wife Livilla. In any case, I supported Sejanus against my own son, and I will never forgive myself for that.

"And then Germanicus died in Syria! He was only 33 years old – the same age as Alexander the Great, and much was made of that. People behaved as if the world was ending – they turned against the gods and threw down their statues! What foolishness! Many accused me of having had him murdered. Would I murder my own nephew, the man chosen by Augustus to succeed me? No, all of this uproar was Agrippina's doing.

"I was genuinely saddened by Germanicus' death, but it did clear the way for Drusus, who was a better soldier and administrator. And Drusus rose to the occasion. He fought brilliantly against the German prince Maroboduus – a very dangerous enemy. I was so proud of him! And even more when his twin sons were born soon after Germanicus died. Surely this would console the people – a new Romulus and Remus!

"Drusus was voted an ovation for his Illyrian victories. Finally, he had emerged from the shadow of Germanicus and come into his own. I knew that the procession through the streets of Rome would mean a great deal to him, so I made it as grand as possible. At last, my own family, my own son, was in the forefront. I wanted Vipsania to share in his crowning moment."

Chapter 49 - Ovation (AD 20)

Tiberius mounted the steps of the temple of Jupiter on the Capitoline hill, where he would view the spectacle of Drusus' ovation. It was the 28th of May – a perfect day – the streets of Rome were lined with the multitudes, gathering to gawk at the young prince and the spoils of his victories. There would be impressive religious observances. There would also be free games, food, and prizes.

Arrayed behind the emperor were the Vestal Virgins, the consuls and other magistrates, and the leading senators with their wives. The buildings were festooned with garlands and ribbons. It was a day to treat a man like a god in recognition of his services to the senate and people of Rome. Tiberius knew how this felt – but it was even better to live it through his son's eyes and ears.

Somewhat to his surprise, Tiberius was overcome with feelings of gratitude and happiness as well as pride. He realized for the first time that he was free. There were no clouds to overshadow him; no Augustus, no Gaius and Lucius, no Germanicus. The world looked only to him, and to his son.

Finally, Drusus rode past the dais, trying to look humble and dignified, but unable to squelch his happy grin. His horse pranced and tossed its mane, expressing the thrill and pride his rider struggled to hide. Tiberius raised his hand in salute and nodded at Drusus, his eyes glistening with tears. Drusus returned the salute and beamed at Vipsania, who was also overcome by the moment.

Gallus sat at her side, trying not to look as glum as he felt. But he could not conceal his shock and fury when Tiberius walked towards him, extended his hand to Vipsania, and escorted her to the front of the porch. The crowd erupted in a deafening cheer for the young Caesar and his parents. Gallus was forgotten, irrelevant. For this moment, Vipsania belonged to Tiberius once again.

For Tiberius, a thousand wounds were being healed – the moment could not be allowed to pass. He looked at Vipsania and made a decision. Whatever the political cost, whatever people might say, she was his wife. She would be his empress. The charade was over – Gallus would have to let her go.

He offered his own chair to Vipsania and then sat beside her. Very few understood the significance of this gesture, but Gallus was one of them. Murderous thoughts swirled through his mind. He would not bear this humiliation!

Tiberius spoke to Vipsania as they received the acclaim of the mob. He had to shout in order to be heard – it felt wonderful to say it out loud. "Do you see how much power they have given us, Vipsania? I did not want it, but I have it nonetheless. What shall I do with so much power? There is only one thing that I want. But I will not take it. Only you can give it to me. Will you be my wife again?"

She surveyed the scene before her. She felt the breath of a quarter million cheering Romans, she saw the sunlight sparkling from the shields and spear points of 10,000 soldiers, the trumpets blaring in time with her heart. It seemed that the stars had aligned themselves in their favor at last.

Vipsania felt love as well as power behind Tiberius' question. There was only one possible answer. She smiled at him and nodded gently. Suddenly, the cheers seemed to swell and acknowledge the moment, the greatest moment in their lives.

Drusus couldn't keep his eyes off of them. He could see that something wonderful had happened, but he was too preoccupied with his own glory to wonder what it was.

When they left the porch, Tiberius still holding Vipsania's hand, Gallus stormed after them, snarling under his breath. "Woman! Have you no shame? Come away at once!" Vipsania paused. They did not turn to face Gallus, nor did they look at each other. They simply froze.

Gallus berated Vipsania: "You've never been a proper wife to me, always thinking of him. I won't have it! I could have you flogged for this!"

Tiberius had had enough. He turned and faced Gallus, towering over him, his guards at the ready. "Silence! She is with me now. You will let her go or feel my wrath!"

Gallus was not cowed. He seethed back at him: "You call yourself a champion of the law, of liberty. You are a tyrant, a despot with no respect for propriety!"

Tiberius knew he spoke the truth this time. He didn't care. He would do this because he could do this. Rome owed him this much.

Vipsania knew that she belonged with Tiberius. She had to be true to him and to her own heart, but she could not bear to be separated from her family in this way. She whispered to Tiberius, "I will come soon. I promise. Give me a few days to make my peace with my children, and with Gallus."

She gently broke away and addressed them both: "I am not a captive, to be bought and sold. I can be with whomever I choose. But I will not make my choice in public!"

Vipsania left with Gallus, but he knew it was no victory.

Chapter 50 - Making Arrangements

Tiberius swept through the halls of his half-finished palace, a small army of artists and architects in his wake.

"These will be the rooms of the lady Vipsania. They must be decorated simply, but elegantly, and with the very finest of materials."

He turned to a bearded Greek man wearing a tunic soiled with the colors of paint. "I want the walls of this room to be decorated with pastoral landscapes; a bucolic paradise. The scenes should be so realistic and detailed that one's eyes can roam in them for hours."

He went into another room with a window balcony. "This chamber will contain marble busts of her father and her mother. Also Atticus and Cicero. Drusus, of course. They should all be life-size and of the very finest workmanship."

Tiberius imagined Vipsania inhabiting these spaces, always near him. His heart had never been so full.

In the house of Gallus, Vipsania was holding court with her children. They were all grown now, her youngest son sixteen and wearing his manly toga. They knew that she would choose Tiberius. They knew that she loved him, though she had never said it. The older boys were more than reconciled to the change by the career advantages it would bring. For all of the children - knowing how ill-suited their parents had been for each other - this would be a relief in some ways. Vipsania scanned their anxious faces and read their thoughts.

"In my heart, I only have one family. And each of my children has an equal share of my thoughts and affection. That will never change. I will always be your mother. My room will always be a haven for each of you; my arms always open to you and to your children. Nothing will change between us. Nothing."

There was a sigh and an easing of tension. Vipsania smiled: "Your father married me so that all of you would benefit from my connections. Now my connections will mean even more."

Downstairs, Gallus was conferring with Syriacus in the courtyard. He held a dagger and repeatedly jabbed it into a wooden bench. "I *cannot* let him take her from me, Syriacus. How could I face the other senators? Or look the bastard in the eye, knowing that he sleeps with my wife! This cannot happen. It *will* not happen."

"There is no way to stop it, my friend. He is the emperor. And you know what Vipsania wants. But think, man, your sons will do very well by this. They will be the sons of the empress!"

Gallus stabbed the bench again, leaving the blade embedded in the wood. "I don't care anymore. I will not let that man triumph over me! I'll do anything to stop him."

Syriacus pulled the dagger free and turned away. "Anything?"

————

The next morning, Drusus jogged through the palace, looking for Tiberius. At every turn, painters and laborers got in his way. He brushed them aside in his haste, spilling bowls of plaster, calling out loud: "Father!"

At last he found him, bent over a table that was covered with building plans. Tiberius turned and saw that his son was distraught. He grabbed his arms: "What has happened, Drusus? What is the matter?"

"Mother! She is very ill! She took sick after dining yesterday evening. I have just come from her. She is in convulsions. Her skin is ashen. The doctors cannot explain it."

————

Alcinous hung his head, his hands folded between his knees. Tiberius paused as he remembered that day and wiped the tears from his face. It took several minutes for the emperor to collect himself.

"When I found her, she was almost gone. She looked so delicate, like a small child, or a half-drowned kitten. I was afraid to touch her, but she gripped my hand with surprising strength. 'It is not his fault! I ate too freely, Tiberius. There was so much excitement.'

"I understood her fears. She knew that she would not recover. She thought that I would blame Gallus and punish his family.

"I asked the doctor, 'Where *is* Gallus?' He replied, 'He has left, Caesar. He says that she is now in your care.'

"I leaned close to her. 'Vipsania, do not be afraid. I know that he would not harm you,' I said, believing it.

"She looked into my soul and whispered: 'Oh my love, can the gods really be so cruel?'

"I kissed her hand and said, 'The gods can do nothing – it is the stars. They cross us at every turn of our lives.' But she was already gone.

"I thought that if I didn't move, if I didn't breathe, that it wouldn't be real. That time would cease and the universe would dissolve. That everything would fall away and only Vipsania would remain, immortal. But I had to breathe, and it all fell in on me, burying my heart. I have never dug myself out. I have been a shade ever since.

"I realized that, even when life seemed hopeless, it was always the hope of Vipsania that had made me carry on. Now, all hope was gone. I could never be happy again.

"I retired. I went to Campania and left Drusus in charge at Rome. I said that I was ill. It was true, my heart and soul were afflicted. I had never known such pain. There were troubles in Germany, Gaul, Spain – I didn't care. The empire could have fallen around my ears and I wouldn't have noticed – Vipsania was dead.

"I returned to Rome more than a year later when Livia was seriously ill. She was 79 years old by this time. I expected her to die, but she didn't. Somehow, this stirred me from my grief. I realized that none of us would live forever and that we should honor those we love while we can.

"Vipsania's two eldest sons, Drusus and Gaius Asinius Pollio, were elected to serve together as consuls for the year after her death. Vipsania received every honor that I dared bestow. I would not allow her to be remembered as a member of the family of Gaius Asinius Gallus. Henceforth, she would be known as the wife of Tiberius Augustus Caesar and the mother of Drusus Caesar. Her image would adorn the ancestral shrines of the Julii and the Claudii - not the Asinii. Her statues would be erected in monuments to the imperial family throughout the empire.

"Drusus struck coins with her image, honoring Pietas, the symbol of devotion to family, country, and the gods. The senate struck coins in honor of the earthquake relief, which I welcomed as a memorial to her goodness. And I struck coins honoring my mother.

"These were only small gestures, but they brought some comfort - to everyone but Gallus. Vipsania could not leave him while she lived, but she would be remembered as my wife and not his. I saw to that. And her coins and statues would always be there to remind him."

Chapter 51 - Aftershocks (AD 23)

Tiberius stretched his legs and clasped his hands behind his head, closing his eyes as he spoke. "But my sorrows were not over when Vipsania died. Just three years later, I lost Drusus. His illness was much like his mother's, only more gradual in its progress.

"I found him lying down in his bed, choking, struggling to breathe. His wife watched from a distance, a cold expression on her face. Suddenly, he exhaled at length – and he didn't breathe again.

I walked to a marble statue of Jupiter in the corner of the room, picked up a bronze lamp stand, and struck the statue, knocking its head off. I wondered if it was a family curse, and wished that I had been the one stricken, rather than the one left behind to mourn.

"And, soon after that, one of my little grandsons passed away. These blows would have killed me, were I not already dead."

Tiberius looked very old, very feeble. The agonies of remembrance were etched on his face. Alcinous interrupted: "Caesar, perhaps you wish to rest now?"

"Yes, you are right. I must pause and recover from the memories, even as I paused and recovered from the events. But recovery is never complete. Not from blows like these."

Alcinous grabbed a torch and made his way through the darkness to his quarters. He paused and listened to the breakers far below. He understood why Tiberius had come to Capri. There was some comfort in isolation. When a man is run over by chariot after chariot, he must get out of the road to tend his wounds.

A few hours later, Tiberius was awakened by a nudge. He rubbed the sleep from his eyes and turned over. She was leaning over his bed. Vipsania smiled at him, she placed her warm hand on his cheek.

He was amazed. She spoke softly, "My darling, it has been so long. I have missed you so much."

He peeled back his blanket and she laid beside him. She stroked his chest and his arms. She kissed his brow sweetly, and then his lips. "But you haven't aged!" he whispered. "I have grown so old and you haven't changed. Where have you been all these years?"

"Always in the next room, my dear. Always listening. I have been waiting for you."

He was so calm, so peaceful with her beside him. He drifted into a blissful, healing slumber. Then he awoke. He sat up and gathered the moment.

"A dream!" he said aloud. He thought to himself, "I don't care if it was a dream. It was real. I am still tingling. I can still taste her. Perhaps *this* is the dream."

Chapter 52 - Helena's Fountain (A. D. 20s)

After her visit to Sardis, Vipsania had corresponded often with the priestess Melissa - to follow up on the earthquake relief and for news of Helena and her family. She provided money through the temple for her daughter's dowry and whatever special needs she might have. When Vipsania passed away, she left a large sum to the temple treasury with the understanding that Helena would continue to be looked after and given funds when she needed them.

Helena's memories of her mother's visit remained vivid, but as they had parted with the certainty they would never meet again, there was little sense of loss when Vipsania died. To Helena, her natural mother seemed distant and unreal – someone she had known but not known. This began to change a few years after Vipsania's death.

When her brother Drusus died, the people of Sardis voted to erect a monument to Rome and the imperial family. It would be a columned *nymphaeum,* a public fountain decorated with statues of Roma, the two recently dead Caesars, Drusus and Germanicus, and their wives, parents, and imperial grandparents. Life-like portraits were commissioned for all of these personages - including Vipsania, who had been restored to the imperial family.

Helena was deeply moved as she watched the monument take shape. When her mother's portrait was unveiled, it was as if Vipsania had come back into her life. The statue became her confidante and refuge. At times it seemed to smile or weep or follow Helena's movements as she walked by. And the statue of Tiberius, with its haughty but serenely benevolent expression, made Helena feel closer to him. She gazed for many hours on his face, wondering what his voice sounded like, wondering if he knew that she existed.

Sometimes, Helena entertained fantasies of seeing her father, of introducing her children to him. She imagined the opportunities they would have as grandchildren of the Roman emperor. But then she would remember Vipsania's warnings. These seemed to be confirmed by the early deaths of Drusus and her cousin Germanicus. Nevertheless, a desire to see her father took shape in her heart, and grew into a longing.

Chapter 53 - Marry Whom? (AD 26)

Tiberius came early to Alcinous' room. The young man was surprised. "I cannot wait for evening. I want to carry on with the story. There isn't much time left, and I cannot leave the monsters unpunished."

Alcinous followed him to the baths, where Tiberius dismissed the attendants. The two men swam and paddled about, nibbling a light breakfast. Finally Tiberius spoke.

"After Vipsania was gone, the world seemed to go mad. Life in Rome was an obscene farce. I wanted to tell everyone, 'Don't you see? Vipsania is gone; nothing matters anymore.' But they insisted on taking life seriously and causing me endless trouble.

"The strangest moment of all was when Agrippina asked for permission to marry Gallus. Can you imagine? The two people I detested most in the world, together?

"She made her case: 'Vipsania's children are my nephews and nieces. I need a husband. Who better than my brother-in-law?'

"Why not the Parthian king, I thought to myself. He would be just as eager to cast me aside! But all she got from me was silence.

"Agrippina was relentless. She pressed me to advance her sons, which I was already doing. Her oldest boy Nero was nearing 20 by now – I knew that she could hardly wait for him to succeed me. She would stop at nothing to see her family on the throne. So I left Rome and I let Sejanus deal with her."

Tiberius laughed from the pit of his stomach. "How it must have aggravated her! She knew that I would hesitate to persecute the daughter of Agrippa and widow of Germanicus, but Sejanus had no such compunctions. He was firmly aligned with her rival Livilla, Drusus' widow. Sejanus had no desire to see Agrippina's family succeed.

"How I laughed when I thought of the plots and counterplots that were turning Rome upside down! I knew that Sejanus could handle it for me, with his praetorians, so I enjoyed my leisure - first at my villas in Campania, then here on Capri. She couldn't touch me – Sejanus saw to that.

"I've never returned to Rome, did you know that? Not even when my mother died. Not even when Agrippina was sent into exile.

"At that time, I really thought the story was over. Vipsania and I were the victims of destiny, and that was all. But I was wrong – the pantomime had just begun. Penelope's suitors were about to discover that Odysseus had returned!"

Tiberius resumed his laughter. Alcinous was bewildered. Tiberius waved at him, trying to catch his breath. "No, my friend, I am not going mad. You will understand soon enough."

Chapter 54 - Bygones (AD 30)

"It all began with Gallus. As you know, he had made a career of frustrating my policies and embarrassing me in the senate. And when Agrippina asked for my permission to marry him, I suspected him of even grander designs. So imagine my astonishment when I heard that he had taken the senate floor and called on me to accuse Agrippina openly for plotting my overthrow!

"I was angry at first. Once again, Gallus was putting me on the spot, knowing full well that I preferred to let the senate handle such matters without my interference. But Sejanus explained to me that Gallus meant well, that he had had a change of heart and was now cooperating with him in rooting out subversives. On several occasions, Gallus surprised everyone by speaking on behalf of Sejanus and my policies.

"'He can be a valuable ally, Caesar,' Sejanus told me. 'He is known as your antagonist, so his support will be taken all the more seriously. In fact, I think you should reward him and encourage him.'

"Do you see what I mean about the world going mad, Alcinous? 'Reward and encourage *Gaius Asinius Gallus?!!*' I knew that Gallus must have had ulterior motives for switching sides, but I did want to support Sejanus in his work.

"I said, 'I will not give him a second consulship, if that is what you have in mind!' 'No, nothing like that is necessary,' Sejanus replied. 'Just have him to dinner and let bygones be bygones. Since the exile of Agrippina, he has been half-expecting a knock on the door in the middle of the night.'

"It was bitter medicine that he prescribed. But dinner with Gallus would not kill me, so I invited him to dine at Spelunca, my villa on the coast south of Rome."

———

Gallus was impressed beyond words. Tiberius had converted a natural cave by the sea into a fantastic Homeric gallery. There were pools and fountains, and awe-inspiring sculptural groups created by the master sculptors of Rhodes. There was Odysseus with the dead Achilles, the monster Scylla attacking Odysseus' ship, Diomedes grasping the *Palladium*, a sacred statue of Athena. And in the back of the cave was a colossal group of the drunken *cyclops* Polyphemus being attacked by Odysseus and his men.

Tiberius greeted Gallus warmly and explained the statues in detail, then led him to a marble table at the feet of Polyphemus. Thrasyllus joined them for the meal, and the wine began to flow. The mood was conciliatory and relaxed, as if they were a group of lawyers having a drink after a contentious court case.

Tiberius complained about his responsibilities. He gestured at Polyphemus, towering above them: "The principate is a one-eyed monster. It eats you alive. I tell you, if it had one eye, I'd poke it out!"

Gallus, at ease and a little drunk, laughed and nodded sympathetically. Tiberius put his hand on his shoulder and continued. "And you have made my task more difficult, Gallus, you know that." Gallus tensed slightly, but the emperor slapped his back and carried on in a friendly manner.

"But now you are supporting Sejanus and cooperating with our policies. At long last, we should be friends, Gallus. You and I remember the old days. We have been through a lot together."

Tiberius hoisted his cup, "To our friendship!" Gallus raised his cup and the two men drank even more deeply.

Gallus spoke seriously of Sejanus. "I resented him at first, I admit. I don't approve of upstarts having too much power any more than you do, Tiberius. But Sejanus has talent. I see that now. He is necessary."

"And he saved my life!" gushed Tiberius. "Right here in this cave! You must have heard about it?" Gallus nodded. "There was a terrible rock fall, right over there (the emperor pointed), and Sejanus placed his body over mine, to take the blows for me."

"Yes, he has great courage, and affection for you, too. Of course… where would he be if you were dead?"

Tiberius scowled. "And where would he be if *he* were dead? You are too cynical, my friend. I'm surprised Vipsania didn't weed that out of you in all those years."

Gallus winced. "As you well know, Tiberius, Vipsania and I were not close. It was a useful marriage. We did our duty to each other. She gave me sons and connections; I protected her. But we were very different in our tastes and attitudes."

Tiberius drifted in his thoughts for a moment, then raised his cup again, "To Vipsania! The most wonderful woman who ever lived!"

Gallus toasted and laughed, as if it was a joke. He could not imagine a man feeling for a woman the way Tiberius felt for Vipsania. He remembered her fondly for a moment, but he couldn't resist...

"Yes, she was an adequate wife. In thirty years of marriage, she only disappointed me once."

"Yes?"

"Oh, it was many years ago. In Ephesos, when I was governor of Asia. My duties required us to be apart for several months. While I was touring the province, she became pregnant. I knew it wasn't mine. No doubt she was lonely while I was away. A girl was eventually born, in Sardis."

His words hung in the air like smoke.

Tiberius was suddenly sober. He realized that he was the father of this child. The sounds of the sea, the birds, the fountains – all disappeared. He heard only Gallus' words, echoing in his brain.

"And what of the child?"

"Exposed, naturally. There were others who knew that it couldn't be mine. Had to be hushed up, for her sake as well as my own. Of course, she was very upset. But my punishment was mild. Syriacus told me to beat her with rods, but I only had her flogged, and not very harshly."

Tiberius became nauseous. His hands closed into fists, trembling on the table. "Did the child survive?"

Gallus was looking at his cup; oblivious of the change in Tiberius' countenance: "I'm certain it perished. Vipsania placed a pendant around her neck, a Trojan horse! Can you imagine anyone on the Trojan side of the Aegean accepting *a gift bearing a Trojan horse?"* He laughed coarsely at his own joke.

Tiberius rose stiffly from his seat, his fists trembling at his sides. He wanted to throttle the man, but he knew he would only kill him. That would be too quick. He thought of Vipsania's suffering. By Jupiter, Gallus would suffer, too!

He signaled the guards and ordered them to arrest Gallus. He scribbled on a piece of paper as he spoke: "Take this man into custody and take this letter to the senate immediately – I want it read publicly at once."

Gallus was in shock. "What are you charging me with?"

Tiberius was affectedly vague as he wrote. "Oh, let's see, of being jealous of my friendship with Sejanus. Yes, that's right. Even though you also have famous friends, like Syriacus."

Tiberius spat on the marble floor and then continued. "Of trying to cozy up to my prefect in the hopes of turning me against him, since I despise you so much. Also of 'misdemeanors'… to be investigated when I come to Rome."

Gallus was trembling. "But you haven't set foot in Rome in four years! When will my trial be held?"

Tiberius handed the note to an officer. "Has it been that long? Well, one of these days."

The soldiers hurried Gallus off. Tiberius called after them, "He must not be allowed to harm himself, do you understand?"

After Gallus was gone and his shouts could no longer be heard, Thrasyllus asked: "Will you search for the girl?"

There was a pause. "And condemn her to a fate like her mother's? She is better off unknown, if she lives."

Tiberius had to cool off and think. He plunged into the grotto pool. His mind drifted back to a series of memories. He remembered Vipsania once saying that she had ten children, instead of nine. And how rejuvenated she had been by her trip to Asia. She told him that she had befriended a young woman there, the daughter of a shepherd. How delighted she was with this woman, and with her child.

But why didn't she tell me? He wondered…and then he understood. Because she knew I would punish Gallus. "And I will!" he said out loud. But his anger quickly subsided into joy as he realized: "We have a daughter! She is happy. Vipsania lives in her!" Tiberius laughed out loud and splashed away like a young dolphin.

———

Almost as an afterthought, Tiberius described the end of Syriacus: "Soon after this, I had him brought to Capri and thrown from the high cliff. He said nothing when I gave the order. He looked below him and wet himself. Then he closed his eyes and I gave the signal. I was asked later what his crime had been, for the record. 'He was a friend of Gallus' was all I said in reply. That was enough."

Alcinous struggled to maintain a blank expression, but Tiberius read it. "Thrasyllus told me you are a Buddhist at heart. I suppose you don't believe in revenge?"

"I believe that anger and spite disturb the mind; make it hard to live philosophically."

Tiberius chuckled. "You may be right, but failure to do my sacred duty to my family also disturbs my mind. I could not explain my actions publicly, of course. I could not reveal Vipsania's adultery, my defiance of Augustus, the existence of our daughter. So I had to dissimulate. That has earned me my reputation as a deranged tyrant, but also the satisfaction that I have avenged the injuries to my family, and to me. That is the Roman way, Alcinous. Like it or not."

Chapter 55 - Sejanus Undone (AD 31)

A year had passed since the arrest of Gallus. Tiberius was buoyed by the knowledge that he had a daughter, living in the East somewhere. Also by the fact that both Gallus and Agrippina were languishing in prison.

Sejanus had recently returned from Rome and was just finishing his business with the emperor. He gathered his scrolls as Tiberius slipped his signet ring back on his finger.

"Caesar, there is one other matter - the usual entreaty from Asinius Gallus." The prefect mocked him, assuming a high, plaintive voice: "What is my crime? When will I be tried? Etcetera, etcetera."

Tiberius grunted. Sejanus hesitated, then spoke: "I must say, Caesar, I think you have shown remarkable leniency in his case."

Tiberius responded absentmindedly, "You do?"

"Yes. I mean - I know that you loved her above all others."

There was an awkward pause. Tiberius became interested: "I'm surprised that you knew about it. Who told you?"

"It's my business to know these things, Caesar."

Tiberius was intrigued. "When did you find out?"

"I learned it from Syriacus, several months before Gallus was arrested. I thought it would be useful in bringing Gallus under control, and I was right. But I regret that it took me almost 10 years to discover the murder."

There was silence. Tiberius picked up a dagger and toyed with it. *"Ten years? Murder?"*

"Of the worst kind, Caesar. To poison his own wife, just to keep you from having her? Why, that's more than murder, that's treason!"

Tiberius could hear his own blood boiling, rumbling like thunder in his brain. Vipsania? His beloved, sweet, gentle Vipsania, poisoned?

Tiberius tried to hide his reaction. There was a darkening of his countenance, and a gripping of the dagger until his knuckles grew white.

Finally, he blurted out: "Here is my response to Gallus: Inform his jailors that he is to be given only the smallest possible quantities of the coarsest, most tasteless, filthiest food they can find. Warm polluted water only to drink. Just barely enough food and water to keep him alive, you understand, but not enough to give him satisfaction or vigor."

Tiberius was shaking violently, his words expelled with great exertion. "His accommodations are to be as uncomfortable and unattractive as possible, cold in winter, hot in summer. No blankets or mattress. He is to have no visitors other than his guards. His trial will commence when I come to Rome."

He looked directly at Sejanus. "I know there are always rumors that I am coming to Rome. Keep them current – and make certain that Gallus hears them all!"

Sejanus nodded, *"Do* you plan to come to Rome soon?" "No!"

Thrasyllus took Sejanus by the arm and escorted him to the door. "Thank you, Sejanus." He whispered to him, "It is still very painful for him to remember. You understand." Sejanus nodded, reassured. He saluted the emperor, and left.

Tiberius fell to his knees in paroxysms of grief and anger. Then he rolled onto his side and sobbed. Loudly at first; then only whimpers. Thrasyllus carefully removed the dagger from his hand.

An hour went by. Thrasyllus waited, afraid to leave him alone with this news. Finally, Tiberius pulled himself onto a chair. He looked at Thrasyllus, who asked in a quiet voice: "What will you do now?"

Tiberius heaved up his words: "To the man who hid the murder of Vipsania from me so that he could blackmail Gallus to do his own bidding? What else does he hide from me? Whom else does he control? The Praetorian Guard is his. He is betrothed to my son's widow. I thought that he, of all men, was my friend. Someone I could trust."

Tiberius stared vacantly at the wall. "Vipsania, poisoned. Because of me. Because I wanted her." He dissolved again into bitter tears.

Tiberius looked at Alcinous. "But how could I remove Sejanus from power? I myself had made him almost unassailable. He had his enemies, of course, but they would just as soon chuck me out with him."

"There was only one person I could trust. One person who had the moral authority and connections with the opposition: my sister-in-law Antonia, the mother of Germanicus. She was admired by everyone, including Agrippina's supporters, and she hated Sejanus."

"I needed an excuse to bring Sejanus down. I knew that with a hint from me, Antonia would provide one, and rally support to my cause at the highest levels. So I wrote her a letter:

"'My dear sister, I have heard reports that Sejanus has exceeded his mandate. That he binds important men and the Praetorian Guard to himself rather than to me. I have been away from Rome for so long that I do not know what to believe. Do you think him capable of plotting against me? Do you think I will find support in Rome if I am forced to depose him? Take care, my dear Antonia, in how you answer me. He reads my incoming mail. Have a servant carry your response to me by hand and deliver it in secrecy. I rely on you to tell me the truth.'

"Her response was exactly what I needed. She said that there was indeed evidence that Sejanus was planning my overthrow, and that his conspiracy included several senators and officers of the Praetorian Guard. This allowed me to remove him without any reference to Vipsania. I struck swiftly, using Macro and his influence with the guardsmen.

"Sejanus was executed. His statues were defaced or removed and his name was stricken from the public monuments. Antonia was toasted as the savior of Rome. My escape from danger was celebrated throughout the empire.

"But this brought me no joy. I was still reeling from the discovery of Vipsania's murder and the loss of a man I trusted and relied upon.

"And this was only the beginning. The pieces of my broken heart would be ground into fragments by what I learned in the next few months. The world no longer seemed mad to me; it seemed evil, evil beyond my worst imaginings."

Chapter 56 - Apicata

The fall of Sejanus drenched Rome with blood. The prefect had held a death grip on many of the noble families, through blackmail and bullying. Now that it was loosened, vengeance was taken against his adherents and family members. His uncle was killed, many of his closest friends committed suicide, many others were lynched. The praetorian guardsmen ran amuck through the city, burning and looting as they went.

Less than a week after Sejanus' death, his son was executed. Devastated by the loss of her child, Sejanus' former wife Apicata committed suicide. Apicata had been cast aside by Sejanus in anticipation of his marriage to Livilla, the widow of Drusus. Now, as her final act, she took her revenge.

It came in the form of a letter to Tiberius, claiming that Drusus had been poisoned by Livilla and Sejanus, assisted by her doctor Lygdus and by Drusus' taster and favorite eunuch, Eudemus. It also charged that Sejanus and Livilla had been lovers while Drusus was still alive.

As he read Apicata's letter, Tiberius' mind reeled. "Drusus must have suspected. That is why he hated Sejanus so much."

Tiberius thought to himself, "I will surely go mad if I do nothing about this. Justice is the only cure for Rome's shame, for my shame!"

He ordered an immediate investigation of the whole matter, to be supervised by himself. "Lygdus and Eudemus shall be arrested and brought here immediately. Every scrap of paper belonging to Drusus, to Livilla, to Sejanus, to Apicata will be brought to me at once! Any informer who can provide verifiable information will be rewarded. I will not rest until I have understood *everything!*"

For weeks, Tiberius remained obsessed with the crimes of Sejanus and Livilla. He rarely ate or slept. He pursued the truth with the same relentless energy with which he once pursued Germans.

Lydgus and Eudemus were subjected to torture – both confessed to their parts in the crime. Livilla herself was referred to her mother Antonia for punishment. Antonia knew what was expected of her in order to preserve the dignity of her family: Livilla was slowly starved to death. The remaining two children of Sejanus and Apicata were executed a month after their parents' deaths.

But Tiberius was not through. He would not rest until he had inspected every scrap of evidence he could lay his hands on. In order to cleanse Rome and assuage Tiberius' guilt, no accomplice could be allowed to go undiscovered or unpunished.

————

Alcinous was stunned by this account, but Tiberius didn't bother to notice or explain. He described his vengeance with gusto – it was his duty and therefore his pleasure to bring down the enemies of his family. But his mood suddenly changed as he turned to a different subject.

"During the course of my investigation, while looking through my son's papers, I found something extraordinary. It was a wooden chest that had once belonged to Vipsania. It was filled with papers, letters, household accounts, but Thrasyllus noticed that the inside of the chest was too shallow; there was a false bottom! Underneath were her personal letters.

"I put them aside until I could give them time. When I did read them, I was amazed. She had kept my letters from Germany and Illyria, even the ones I wrote from Spain and Armenia before we were married. There were passages from me asking about Drusus when he was an infant, and promising her my undying love, just weeks before Augustus made me divorce her. I wept over each one and threw it into the fire. No one else would ever see these precious things. No one.

"But there were other letters, too. From her friend in Ephesos, the priestess, telling her about our daughter Helena in Sardis. I was thrilled to read this – I knew her name at last, and where she lived. This confirmed what I already believed – Vipsania must have seen her in Sardis during the earthquake mission.

"But there was one letter I did not understand. It was in Greek and it was not signed. The letters were large and coarse and the meaning was hard to decipher. It said: 'A man you know and respect has come to you. You will pay him what he requested. Do not think that distance has changed things.'

"What could this letter mean? And who wrote it? For many days, I had no clue. But finally the affair of Drusus' murder began to release my mind and I made some progress. 'The letter is in Greek and from far away. Money is involved, and Vipsania is being forced to pay it against her will. Blackmail! But what could Vipsania have to hide? Helena? My visit to see her in Ephesos? But who could know these things?'

"I reasoned further. 'Perhaps someone saw us together in Ephesos, or knew about the baby – or knew that I left Rhodes to see her.' I remembered my enemies in Rhodes and I wondered.

"My brain began to ache over the matter. How could I ever discover the blackmailer? I looked through Vipsania's papers again, looking for evidence. A random thought flew into my head like a bee in a helmet.

"I ordered my secretary to bring the documents that I had made the Rhodians sign soon after Augustus' death, to correct their omissions."

Alcinous came to attention.

"Yes, that's right! I recognized the handwriting. The same big stubby letters – it was Eurymachos!"

Chapter 57 - Justice (AD 32)

Eurymachos had no idea why the emperor had summoned him. It had been 30 years since Tiberius left Rhodes, and almost two decades since Eurymachos had last seen him in Rome. Perhaps the old man was lonely and wanted to remember his Rhodian days? It didn't seem possible that Tiberius had learned about the blackmail. Vipsania was long dead – how could he have discovered it now?

The summons was certainly cordial enough: "Come to Capri and let me repay your hospitality," the letter said. Nothing ominous in that. In fact, Eurymachos was confident enough to boast to the sailors that he knew the emperor when he was a vagabond: "Why he was even a tenant in one of my houses!"

When Eurymachos arrived, he was immediately seized by two guards who didn't speak Greek, so they wouldn't understand the conversation.

At Tiberius' signal, they softened him up with some blows to his midsection. Eurymachos glared at the emperor defiantly, looking innocent – until Tiberius dangled the letter to Vipsania in front of his face.

Eurymachos was stunned but indignant: "Caesar, that was thirty-five years ago!"

Tiberius was unmoved. Eurymachos saw that his life was over, so he was determined to take as many Romans with him as he could.

"It was your friends! Flaccus and Marinus! It was all their idea. They suggested I follow you to Ephesos. Romans should never be trusted!"

Tiberius scoffed at him: "Whereas Greeks like you are completely honest? Who else was involved? Who was your contact in Rome?"

"It was another Roman, a senator – Sextus Vestilius. Flaccus knows him."

Tiberius was surprised and saddened. Sextus was an old friend from his army days, close to his brother Drusus. The emperor nodded to the guards, who tossed the screaming Eurymachos from the cliff.

At this point, Macro appeared, looking confused, running up to Tiberius. "Caesar, who was that man?"

"A witness in the case of my son's murder."

Shaking his head, Macro replied: "No, Caesar, he wasn't. I am certain he wasn't."

Tiberius turned away to hide his grin: "Whoops!!!"

To Alcinous' disgust, Tiberius laughed out loud and repeated his reply over and over, each time in a sillier voice. "Whoops! *Whooops! Whoooooopsssss!*"

Alcinous could not share the joke.

Tiberius gathered himself and leaned forward. "You must understand, Alcinous. This man caused my Vipsania much pain and anxiety. She did not know that he wouldn't report us to Augustus, or to Gallus. He could have ruined both of us. She had to live with that uncertainty. Besides, blackmail is a crime and he deserved to be punished for it."

Satisfied with this, the emperor continued. "The betrayal of Sextus was more troubling to me even that those of Flaccus and Marinus. Here was a man I trusted, whom I had taken into my inner circle after my brother's death. He was often my guest on Capri, so I invited him to visit and began to play with his mind."

———

Sextus' journey to Capri was a hardship. He was not as spry as the emperor and very nearly as old. But Tiberius greeted him warmly and he enjoyed swapping stories of the German wars.

One evening, Sextus attended a banquet given by the emperor in his honor. Flaccus and Marinus were also present, summoned from Rome especially for the occasion. After a great many tall tales and flasks of wine, Sextus began his customary diatribe on the younger generations.

"They lack the self-discipline and courage we had, Tiberius. Men have grown soft because of our victories – we made things too safe for them. If another Maroboduus or Arminius should arise, who would face him?"

Tiberius suddenly became serious. "Yes, Sextus, I have heard what you wrote about Caligula, even though he is my beloved great nephew and the grandson of your friend Drusus. You called him a 'sissy lapdog who couldn't fight his way out of a hairnet.' You said that he 'has made love to more women than Zeus and more men than Aphrodite – and more sheep than the king of the satyrs!'"

Sextus was aghast. He may have thought such things, even said them to close friends, but he would never write them down!

Caligula was present. His temples throbbed. He stood and moved menacingly toward Sextus, who cowered and groaned. "I swear I never wrote such things, Caesar. I swear it!"

Tiberius motioned to Caligula to resume his seat. "What you say may be true, Sextus, but I do not think you should dine with us anymore. You are no longer welcome at my table."

In shock at this sudden turnabout, Sextus withdrew to his room. He considered his situation and decided it was hopeless. Yes, he had spoken against Caligula, and Caligula would soon be emperor, or so it seemed. There was only one honorable course of action. In order to avoid execution and the ruin of his family, he had to take his own life.

His gnarled hand quivering, Sextus sliced his wrists. He dictated letters to his family in Rome and to Tiberius while the blood drained away.

But his letter to Tiberius gave him fresh hope. There was no written document against Caligula. Perhaps if he denied it fervently and humbled himself before the prince, he could escape punishment?

Clinging to this, Sextus bound up his wounds and waited for the emperor's reply to his letter. It arrived as one word scratched on a wax tablet: "Eurymachos."

Sextus knew he was doomed. He reopened his wounds and waited for the end to come.

Meanwhile, at the banquet, Tiberius turned his attention to Flaccus and Marinus. Unnerved by the confrontation with Sextus but too drunk to comprehend its meaning, they suddenly realized the emperor was glaring at them.

"And now, my so-called friends, I have a question for you. Why is it that you loved Eurymachos more than you loved me?"

They were shocked. They tried to stand up and make their escape, but they were too drunk. At Tiberius' signal, the guards grabbed them. With mock concern, the emperor said, "Be careful! You could have a bad fall in that condition. Macro! Take them to the cliff and make sure that they do!"

The Prefect and his guards hustled them to their deaths.

———

"Yes, Alcinous, I was finally able to avenge the wrongs done to Vipsania, to Drusus, to myself - but it broke my heart. These were my oldest friends, or so I had thought – Sejanus, Sextus, Flaccus, Marinus. They all betrayed me.

"The deaths of Agrippina and Gallus in the following year cheered me up a bit. But then my dear friend Cocceius Nerva took his own life by starvation – he would not tell me why. There was only Thrasyllus left, and a world full of clowns."

Chapter 58 - Pity (AD 37)

That night in his room, Alcinous suddenly realized that the story was over. What had begun as a romantic saga of love and courage had ended in an orgy of vengeance.

He felt sorry for Tiberius – what a tragic man! Alone with his bitterness, taking pleasure in the punishment of his former friends.

It was Vipsania who impressed him most. Like Penelope, she never wavered in her devotion to Tiberius. She bore all the pain, loss, humiliation, and anxiety with nobility and self-restraint. Even at her death, she was concerned with protecting others rather than seeking retribution. How different history might have been if such a woman had been empress of Rome, to guide Tiberius and soften his heart!

A few days later, the emperor announced that he was going to Rome. His entourage was assembled and sailed to the mainland where Tiberius, wearing his old general's uniform, mounted his horse. Alcinous remained behind to begin work on his "history," though he would procrastinate on this for a week or more.

As usual, Tiberius sent scouts to deflect onlookers along the way – he did not want to be the object of their curiosity and derision. Seven miles from the capital, he paused to rest. He wanted to look as vigorous and refreshed as possible when he entered the city gates. Two days were spent napping.

It was early afternoon on the third day. Macro entered the emperor's room. He was dozing on a couch. Without opening his eyes, Tiberius said "What do you want, Macro? I am tired."

"Forgive me, Caesar. There is a Greek woman here to see you. She says that she has come to pay her respects. She has brought her son, a good-looking young man."

"You know how I feel about gawkers, Macro. Send her away!"

"She says that you were acquainted with her family, when you were in Rhodes. She asked me to give you this."

Tiberius opened his eyes to see a red carnelian horse dangling from Macro's fist. He swung his legs off the couch and stared at the necklace. A shudder of excitement passed through him. "Yes, I remember her family. I will see them."

Macro turned to usher them in. Tiberius called after him. "Macro!"

"Yes, Caesar?"

"We will want to reminisce. See that we are not disturbed. By anyone."

"Yes, Caesar."

When she entered the room, Tiberius stopped breathing. She had Vipsania's aura and her features. The skin was darker from the sun, the hair looser, the clothes less fine - but the same presence and dignity. Tiberius began to cry. He blubbered out the name "Helena!" and she ran to him. She wrapped her arms around her father for the very first time.

Tiberius eventually pulled himself together and looked into her eyes. His smile was so sweet that she began to cry. Then he looked at his grandson – it was Agrippa's face, with Tiberius' nose. Tiberius laughed and pointed at his own proboscis, then at Telemachos. The young man laughed and moved closer, took his grandfather's hand.

They spoke of Vipsania, of the earthquake, of Helena's remarriage and five children. But the words weren't important. They knew that this was a brief encounter between two worlds that had to remain separate. What mattered and would last was the mingling of tears - and the memories of Vipsania, the sense of her presence in the room.

After an hour or two or more, Macro entered. "Forgive me, Caesar.

There is urgent news from Capri." "What is so urgent?"

"There has been an earthquake. Damage was done to your villa, Caesar. And the lighthouse has collapsed!"

"What a nuisance! I'll build another one."

"There is more. Your pet snake was found dead, half eaten by ants. Perhaps it was frightened to death by the tremors? And that Greek fellow you spent so much time with – Alcinous? He was in the lighthouse when it collapsed. He was killed."
Tiberius was stunned. Then he began to laugh. He dismissed Macro. Helena looked at him in disbelief. She wondered if he laughed at the death

of the snake or the death of the man.

Her father explained. "Do not think me callous, my dear. The man was my friend. So was the snake, come to that.

"I've spent the past few weeks telling Alcinous my story, your mother's story – even your story, what I knew of it. He was going to write it down. But it is just as well. It might have led to your door someday, if anyone believed a word of it."

The time came for Helena and Telemachos to leave. "Will you continue to Rome, father?"

"No, I don't believe I will." He looked lovingly at her, and then at Telemachos.

"I believe that I have now seen all that I will ever want to see. Besides, it has been prophesied that I will never return there. I wouldn't want to disappoint the soothsayers, now would I?"

He kissed Helena tenderly on her forehead, her eyelids, her cheeks. He placed the carnelian horse around her neck. He gripped Telemachos by the shoulders, marveling at his youth and strength. He bid them farewell.

By the time Helena and Telemachos reached the port of Ostia, after a visit to Rome and Vipsania's tomb, the news had already arrived: Tiberius was dead. From the outskirts of Rome, he had journeyed to Astura, where he fell ill. He improved and went on to Cerceii, and even threw javelins at a wild boar in the arena. But then he got a pain in his side, followed by a chill.

He retired to his villa at Misenum and took to his bed. On the 16th of March, he suddenly worsened. He took off his ring - then put it back on his finger. He tried to get out of bed, but collapsed on the floor and died. And now Caligula was the new emperor.

Helena was saddened by the news. She barely knew her father, but her affection for him was real. "I am so glad we saw him..."

Telemachos agreed. "Yes, but I will be glad to be home again. He was once a good man, I believe. But Romans make me nervous. And I would never want to be a Caesar."

AFTERWORD

What romantically inclined reader isn't intrigued by these lines from the Roman historian Suetonius?

"Tiberius married Vipsania Agrippina, the daughter of Marcus Agrippa and the grand-daughter of Caecilius Atticus, the Roman knight to whom Cicero's letters were addressed. After Tiberius had acknowledged as his own the son Drusus that she bore him, although she was a good match for him and was pregnant once again, he was forced to divorce her without delay and to marry Julia, the daughter of Augustus. This caused no small anguish in his heart, both because he was fixed in his devotion to Vipsania and because he disapproved of Julia's conduct - having perceived along with everyone else that she was lusting after him when she was still married to her previous husband. But after the divorce he was grief-stricken over having parted with Vipsania. On one occasion, he caught sight of her and followed her with such eager, tear-filled eyes that a watch was set up to ensure that she would never come into his view again." (Suetonius, *Tiberius VII, 2-3,* translation by James R. Burns)

Added to this is the remarkable coincidence that Tiberius' retirement from the second most important position in the empire and his removal to Rhodes coincided exactly with Vipsania's husband's posting as governor of the province of Asia, just a few miles from that island.

But who is fictional and who is historical in this story? All of the characters in this novel are taken from the pages of history except for Alcinous, Helena and her Asian family, the priestesses Artemis and Melissa, and Gallus' mother Salonina (her actual name and dates are not recorded). The name "Eurymachos" is also imaginary, but represents an unnamed host of Tiberius in Rhodes who was summoned to Capri in AD 32 and executed.

There is no proof that Tiberius visited Vipsania during his time in Rhodes. Her presence in Asia with her husband is probable, given the custom of the time, but not documented. Nor is there any evidence that she visited the province after the earthquake of AD 17. There is no sign that Tiberius and Vipsania had a child after their divorce, nor that Tiberius sought to reunite with his first wife after he became emperor.

However, Vipsania did die in her early 50's "a few days" after Drusus' ovation, though the cause of her death is unknown. Tiberius never remarried after his separation from Julia in about 9 BC. Vipsania was posthumously restored to Tiberius' family and celebrated in imperial monuments throughout the empire. She may also have been honored on coins issued in the name of her son in AD 23, as I have argued elsewhere (see *The Celator: Journal of Ancient and Medieval Coins and Artifacts*, May 2004 - or http://www.jasperburns.com/gasvips.htm).

The dates and general circumstances of the deaths of Gallus, Syriacus, Sextus, Flaccus, Marinus, Sejanus, and "Eurymachos," are all as recorded by the ancient historians. However, the connection of Vipsania to these deaths is entirely conjectural.

More by Jasper Burns

Irish Hammered Pennies of Edward IV and Richard III, 2nd Edition (Pietas Publications, 2014)

Virginia Through Time (Pietas Publications, 2014)

Two Lucys in Europe 1884 (Pietas Publications, 2014)

A Lady in Jamaica 1879 (Pietas Publications, 2014)

Gale Hill: The Story of an Old Virginia Home (Pietas Publications, 2013)

Coin Stories (Pietas Publications, 2013)

Commodus and the Five Good Emperors (Pietas Publications, 2012)

Roman Empresses (Pietas Publications, 2012)

Bulla Felix: The Roman Robin Hood (Pietas Publications, 2011)

Irish Hammered Pennies of Edward IV and Richard III (Pietas Publications, 2009)

Great Women of Imperial Rome: Mothers and Wives of the Caesars (Routledge, 2007)

Trilobites: Common Trilobites of North America (NatureGuide Books, 2000)

Fossil Collecting in the Mid-Atlantic States (Johns Hopkins University Press, 1991)

www.ingramcontent.com/pod-product-compliance
Lightning Source LLC
Chambersburg PA
CBHW051454050726
47593CB00005B/2072